BIGGLES
IN THE ORIENT

'What in the name of all that's unholy brought you to this God-forsaken, sun-blistered dustbin?' inquired Frayle curiously.

'I'm told you've had a spot of trouble here,' replied Biggles. 'I've been sent out from home to try to iron it out.'

'Go ahead,' invited Frayle bitterly. 'The airfield's yours—and you're welcome to it. I've lost four officers and four machines in four days—the last four to go out, in fact. That should encourage you to keep your feet on something more solid than the floor of a fuselage. I've three officers left out of eighteen. Not bad going, eh?'

BIGGLES
IN THE ORIENT

CAPTAIN W. E. JOHNS

RED FOX

Red Fox would like to express their grateful thanks for help in preparing these editions to Jennifer Schofield, author of *By Jove, Biggles*, Linda Shaughnessy of A. P. Watt Ltd and especially to John Trendler, editor of *Biggles & Co*, the quarterly magazine for Biggles enthusiasts.

A Red Fox Book
Published by Random House Children's Books
20 Vauxhall Bridge Road, London SW1V 2SA

A division of Random House UK Ltd
London Melbourne Sydney Auckland
Johannesburg and agencies throughout the world

First published by Oxford University Press 1945

Red Fox edition 1992
Reprinted 1992 (twice)

Set in 10.5/12pt Baskerville
Photoset by Intype, London
Printed and bound in Great Britain
by Cox & Wyman Ltd, Reading, Berkshire

ISBN 0 09 993830 8

Contents

Chapter 1
Outward Bound

With the serene dignity of a monarch bestowing a favour, His Majesty's Flying-boat *Capricorn* kissed the turquoise water of the marine aircraft base at Calafrana, Malta, and in a surge of creamy foam came to rest by her mooring buoy, setting numerous smaller craft bobbing and curtsying in a gentle swell that was soon to die on the concrete slipways. Through the sparkling atmosphere of the Mediterranean dawn every detail of the rockbound coast stood revealed with a clarity unknown in northern isles.

In the cabin, Squadron Leader Bigglesworth, more commonly known to his friends (and, perhaps his enemies) as 'Biggles,' yawned as he stood up and reached for the haversack containing his small-kit that rested on the luggage rack above his seat.

'I've had a nice sleep,' he announced inconsequently, for the benefit of the several officers of his squadron who were pulling on shoes, fastening tunics, and the like, preparatory to disembarking.

It was the same little band of hard-hitting warriors that had fought under him during the Battle of Britain, in the Western Desert, and elsewhere, and more than one carried scars as perpetual souvenirs of these theatres of war. That none had been killed was, admittedly, a matter of wonder. There were some who ascribed this to astonishing good fortune; others, to leadership which combined caution with courage. Other reasons put forward were superb flying, straight shooting, and close co-operation—which is another way of saying that sort of comradeship which puts the team before self. The truth was probably to be found in a combination of all these attributes.

There were the three flight commanders: Algy Lacey, fair and freckled; Lord 'Bertie' Lissie, effeminate in face and manner, for ever polishing an eyeglass for no reason that anyone could discover; and Angus Mackail, twelve stone of brawn and brain, with heather in his brogue and an old regimental glengarry on his head. All wore the purple and white ribbon of the D.F.C.*

The rest were flying officers; like the flight-lieutenants they were all long overdue for promotion, but as this would have meant leaving the squadron (wherein there was no establishment for senior ranks, and consequently no chance of advancement) they had forgone promotion to remain in the same mess. There was 'Ginger' Hebblethwaite, a waif who had attached himself to Biggles and Algy before the war, and who had almost forgotten the slum in which he had been born; 'Tex' O'Hara, a product of the wide open spaces of Texas, U.S.A.; 'Taffy' Hughes, whose paternal ancestor may have been one of those Welsh knifemen that helped the Black Prince to make a name for valour; 'Tug' Carrington, a Cockney and proud of it, handy with his 'dukes,' hating all aggressors (and Nazis in particular) with a passion that sometimes startled the others; Henry Harcourt, a thin, pale, thoughtful-eyed Oxford undergraduate, who really loathed war yet had learned how to fight; and 'Ferocity' Ferris, who, born in a back street of Liverpool, had got his commission, not by accident (as he sometimes said) but by sheer flying ability.

* Distinguished Flying Cross.

This strange assortment of humanity, which could only have been drawn together by the vortex of war, formed Number 666 (Fighter) Squadron, R.A.F. More usually it was referred to in places where airmen meet as 'Biggles' Squadron.' And this was the literal truth, for on the formation of the unit, to Biggles had been sent—with his knowledge, of course—pilots of peculiar temperament, men with only two things in common, utter fearlessness and a disinclination to submit to discipline—two traits that often go together. Nevertheless, by example, by the force of his own personality, and by a strange sort of discipline which appeared to be lax, but was, in fact rigid, Biggles had moulded them into a team with a reputation that was as well known to the enemy as to the Air Ministry. The result was a third common factor—loyalty; loyalty to the service, to the team, and above all, to their leader.

'There's a cutter coming out, presumably to take us ashore,' observed Algy, from a seat that commanded a view of the port. 'Now we shall know what it's all about. I must confess to some curiosity as to the whys and wherefores of this sudden rush to Malta.'

'It isn't customary for an Air Commode* to turn out to meet new arrivals,' remarked Ginger. 'There's an Air Commodore in the stern of that cutter—I can see his scrambled eggs** from here.'

'Maybe it's a new regulation. Welcome to your new home, gentlemen, and all that sort of thing—if you see what I mean?' suggested Bertie, brightly.

A minute later the Air Commodore stepped aboard. He went straight to Biggles, who by this time was

* Slang: Air Commodore.
** Slang: those of the rank of Group Captains and above making reference to the gold braid on the service cap.

looking a trifle surprised at this unusual reception.

''Morning, Bigglesworth,' greeted the Air Commodore.

''Morning, sir,' answered Biggles.

'Everything all right?'

'Why not?' queried Biggles.

'Oh, I don't know,' returned the Air Commodore. 'The Higher Command seems to be particularly concerned about you. You'll find breakfast ready in the mess. Better not waste any time—you've only got an hour.'

The puzzled expression on Biggles' face deepened. 'An hour for what, sir?'

'To stretch your legs, I suppose.'

'But I don't quite understand,' murmured Biggles. 'I was ordered to bring my squadron here. Naturally, I assumed it was for duty on the island.'

'I don't know anything about that,' returned the Air Commodore. 'My orders—by signal received last night—were to give you breakfast and push you along to Alexandria. The aircraft leaves the water in an hour. My tender will take you ashore. You might as well leave your kit where it is.'

'Very good sir.'

The Air Commodore walked forward to speak to the pilot.

'Well, stiffen me rigid!' exclaimed Ginger softly. 'What do you make of that?'

Biggles shrugged. 'I don't make anything of it. We've got our orders. Alex it is, apparently. Let's go ashore for a shower and a rasher of bacon.'

Eight hours later the *Capricorn* touched down in the sweeping bay of Alexandria. Biggles stood up and reached for his haversack.

'Just a minute,' said Ginger. 'There's another brass-hat* in that cutter coming out from station head-quarters.'

Biggles looked through the window. 'You're right,' he confirmed. 'It looks as though the Near East is littered with Air Commodores. Unless I'm mistaken that's Buster Brownlow. He's a good scout. He commanded Ten Group in the Battle of Britain.'

The Air Commodore came aboard.

'Hello, Biggles!' he greeted. 'Get cracking—you've only got an hour.'

Biggles started. 'What, *again*?'

The Air Commodore raised his eyebrows. 'What do you mean—again?'

Biggles laughed shortly. 'Well, last night, out of the blue, I got an order instructing me to hand over my equipment and take the squadron by road to Pembroke Dock, where the *Capricorn* was waiting to take us to Malta. We made our landfall at dawn, after a comfortable trip. The A.O.C., Malta, pushed us along here. Now you're telling us—'

'That you're not stopping. Quite right. There's a Wimpey** on the tarmac waiting to take you to Baghdad, so you'd better get ashore.'

'Do you happen to know what this is all about?' questioned Biggles curiously.

'I know no more than you,' answered the Air Commodore, and returned to the motor-boat.

'Join the Air Force and see the world,' murmured Ferocity Ferris, with bitter sarcasm.

'That's it. The service is living up to its jolly old reputation, what?' remarked Bertie.

---

* Slang: a staff officer, also referring to the gold braid on his service cap.
** A Wellington—Twin engine heavy bomber made by Vickers.

The sun was setting behind the golden domes of Khadamain, the most conspicuous landmark in the ancient city of the Caliphs, when the Wellington rumbled to a stand-still on the dusty surface of Hinaidi airfield, Baghdad.

Biggles stood up. 'Now maybe we shall get the gen* on this circus,' he asserted.

The cabin door was opened and an officer wearing the badges of rank of a Group Captain looked in. 'Get weaving, you fellows,' he called breezily. 'A head wind has put you ten minutes behind schedule. You're moving off in fifty minutes. Leave your kit where it is and stride along to the mess for dinner.'

Biggles frowned. 'What is this—a joke?'

'Joke?' The Group Captain seemed surprised. 'Not as far as I know. What gave you that quaint idea?'

'Only that it's customary for officers to know where they're going,' answered Biggles. 'This morning we were at Malta.'

'Well, by to-morrow morning you'll be in India,' returned the Group Captain. 'My orders are to push you along to Karachi. Someone may tell you why when you get there. See you presently.'

Biggles looked over his shoulder at the officers who, with their kit, filled the cabin. 'You heard that?' he queried helplessly. 'We're on our way to India. The Air Ministry, having decided that we need a rest, is giving us a busman's holiday. If this goes on much longer we shall meet ourselves coming back.'

'I don't get it,' muttered Tex.

'Presumably none of us is supposed to get it,' replied Biggles. 'No doubt we shall though, eventually, if we keep on long enough.'

* Slang: information.

The stars were paling in the sky when, the following morning, the aircraft landed at Drigh Road airfield, Karachi.

'This, I should say, is it,' said Tug confidently.

'I wouldn't bet on it,' murmured Henry Harcourt, moodily.

The pilots stepped down. As they stretched their cramped limbs two jeeps came tearing across the sun parched earth. After they skidded to a stop a Wing Commander alighted.

''Morning Biggles,' he greeted. 'Get your fellows aboard and I'll run you to the mess. Coffee is waiting. You haven't long—'

'Okay, okay, I know,' broke in Biggles impatiently. 'We've only got an hour, then you're pushing us along to—where is it this time?'

'Dum Dum. Our best Liberator* is waiting to take you. Say thank you.'

'Thank you my foot,' snapped Biggles. 'We've been careering round the globe for forty-eight hours. I'm getting dizzy.'

'I thought Dum Dum was a kind of bullet,' grunted Taffy.

'So it is,' answered Biggles. 'It also happens to be an airfield about two miles from Calcutta, on the other side of India. They say that in the old days the first dum-dum bullets were made there. I could use some, right now. Let's go. Even if we're condemned to chase the rainbow we might as well eat.'

It was late in the afternoon when the Liberator landed its load of pilots at Calcutta. Biggles was first out, fully prepared to see a duty officer with a fresh movement order in his hand. Instead, his eyes fell on

---

* A four engine bomber made by Consolidated USA.

the last man he expected to see. It was Air Commodore Raymond, of Air Intelligence, who, as far as he knew, seldom left the Air Ministry.

'Hello,' greeted the Air Commodore with an apologetic smile.

Biggles shook his head sadly. 'I should have guessed it,' he said wearily. 'Was all this rushing from here to there really necessary?'

'You can decide that for yourself, after we've had a chat,' replied the Air Commodore seriously. 'Do you want a rest, or shall we get down to things right away?'

'Is the whole squadron included in that invitation?'

'No. I'd rather talk to you alone in the first place. You can tell your fellows about it later on—in fact, you'll have to. But the Air Officer Commanding, India, and the G.O.C* land forces, are here, waiting to have a word with you. That'll give you an idea of the importance of the matter that caused you to be rushed out.'

'All right, sir. In that case we'd better get down to brass tacks right away. What about my officers?'

'They can go and get settled in their new quarters. Everything is arranged. You've got your own mess.**'

'Then this really *is* the end of the trail?'

'I don't want to seem depressing, but it's likely to be the end of the trail in every sense of the word. We're up against it, Bigglesworth, and when *I* say that you can guess it's pretty bad.'

'So you send for me,' said Biggles plaintively. 'We were supposed to be due for a rest.'

'I didn't send for you,' denied the Air Commodore. 'The A.O.C.*** fixed that with the Ministry.

---

* General Office Commanding.
** Place where the men eat and relax together.
*** Air Officer Commanding.

Admittedly, I mentioned your name. See what comes of having a reputation. Matter of fact, I wasn't pleased myself at being hauled out here — I've been here three days.'

Biggles turned to speak to Algy. 'Take over,' he ordered. 'I'll join you later.'

Without speaking, the Air Commodore led the way to station headquarters, where, in an inner office, the two generals were waiting.

'Sorry to rush you about.like this, Bigglesworth, but there were reasons,' explained the Air Officer, holding out his hand.

Biggles nodded. 'I've been in the service long enough to know that things don't happen without a reason, sir,' he said simply.

'We brought you out here as we did, for two reasons. The first was speed, and the second, security. The fewer people who know you are here, the better. The Japanese High Command knows all about you, so if they learned that you were on the way out they'd put two and two together.' A note of bitterness crept into the Air Marshal's voice. 'They might even have prevented your arrival. Of course they are bound to find out sooner or later, but by that time you'll be on the job — I hope. Take a pew.' The A.O.C. sat down, mopping perspiration from his forehead with a large handkerchief, for the air was heavy and hot. 'Raymond, I think you'd better tell the story,' he suggested.

Chapter 2
Haunted Skies

With cigarettes lighted the four officers sat at a table that was entirely covered by a map of Eastern Asia.

'In this war of wars,' began the Air Commodore, looking at Biggles, 'from time to time one side or the other is suddenly confronted by a new weapon, or device, which, for a while at any rate, seems to defy counter measures. The result is a temporary advantage for the side employing the instrument. Hitler's magnetic and acoustic mines were typical examples. We have given *him* some hard nuts to crack, too. After a while, of course, the mystery is solved, but while it persists the Higher Command gets little sleep. Here, in our war against Japan, we have bumped into something that is not only lifting our casualties to an alarming degree, but is affecting the morale of pilots and air crews, and, indirectly, the troops on the ground in the areas where we are unable to provide adequate air cover.'

'That's unusual,' murmured Biggles.

'Unusual but understandable, as I think you will presently agree,' resumed the Air Commodore. 'British fighting forces are rarely perturbed by odds against them, or any new method of waging war, provided they know what they are fighting against: but when a man is suddenly confronted by the unknown, by something that kills without revealing itself—well, he is to be pardoned if his nerves begin to suffer. As you know, as well as I do, in such circumstances weak characters try

16

to find Dutch courage by ginning-up, drinking more liquor than they can carry; already we have had one or two bad cases. To put the matter bluntly, we have run into something very nasty, and to make matters worse, we haven't the remotest idea of what it is. Of course, the Oriental mind works on different lines from ours, but not even our Eastern experts can hazard a guess as to what is *going* on. And now, before we go any farther, I'll tell you what *is* going on.' The Air Commodore stubbed his cigarette.

'The trouble first occurred on our air route between India and Chungking, in China,' he continued. 'You've probably heard something about that particular line of communication. When the Japs crashed into Burma, and put the Burma Road out of commission, we had to find a new way of getting war material to China. Our answer was a new life-line up the Himalayas to Tibet, and across the Tibetan plateau to China. At first coolies did the work, manhandling the stuff on their backs. But it was slow. To make a long story short we developed an air service, one that kept clear of the northern extremity of Burma, and possibly Japanese interference. For a time all went well; then, for some unaccountable reason, machines failed to get through. Not all of them. Occasionally one went through on schedule, and this only deepened the mystery. Perhaps I had better make the point clear. Naturally, when our machines first started to disappear we assumed that the Japs had got wind of the route and had established an advanced base from which fighters could operate. And that may in fact be the case. But the astonishing thing is, pilots who *have* got through have invariably reported a clear run. They didn't see a single enemy machine the whole way. That's hard to explain. If the Japs know of the route, and are attacking it, it seems extraordinary that some machines should be allowed to pass unmolested. In a nutshell, our machines either got through untouched, or they didn't get through at all. There was nothing in between. What I am trying to make clear is, the machines that failed, disappeared utterly. There has not been a single case of a pilot fighting his way through. In the ordinary course of events one would expect machines to arrive at their destination badly shot up, to report that they had been attacked by enemy fighters. But that has not happened. As I say, once in a while a pilot makes an uneventful flight. The rest just vanish.'

'That certainly is odd,' murmured Biggles. 'What is the position on the route now?'

'Between ourselves, we are temporarily suspending operations. We must. The surviving pilots are getting the jitters, and the commanding officer is jibbing at sending men to almost certain death. In the last few days a number of pilots have volunteered to rush through with some badly needed medical stores. None of them arrived. We can't go on like that.'

'But surely,' interposed Biggles, 'surely with radio a pilot could report the menace the moment it appeared? Whatever the trouble was, he would have warning of it, if only for a few seconds—time enough to flash a signal.'

The Air Commodore nodded. 'I was waiting for you to say that. You've put a finger on the most inexplicable part of the whole business. No such message has ever been received. In every case the radio has gone dead on us. We once sent a machine out with instructions to report to base every five minutes.'

'What happened?'

'The signals came through like clockwork for an hour. Then they just faded out.'

'Good Lord!' Biggles looked amazed. 'No wonder your pilots are getting jumpy. Tell me this. Does the interference apply to both ends of the route?'

'That's another astonishing thing. It doesn't. No machine has ever had the slightest difficulty in getting through from China to India. It's the India-China service that has been cracked up.'

'That certainly is a poser,' muttered Biggles, slowly. 'It doesn't seem to make sense. Have you tried operating at night?'

'We have,' asserted the Air Commodore. 'That was the first counter-measure we tried. It made no difference. Machines disappeared just as regularly as by day.'

Biggles shook his head. 'I don't wonder you're in a flap.'

'But just a minute,' went on the Air Commodore. 'There is worse to come. The same rot has now set in elsewhere, in the regular service squadrons. At the moment four stations are reporting abnormally high casualties without being able to offer the slightest explanation. In each case the casualty is a complete disappearance. The second place to suffer was right here, at Dum Dum. The third was Trichinoply, Madras, halfway down the coast, and the fourth, Ceylon, at the tip of the peninsula.'

'From which we may suppose that the Japs, perceiving that they are on a winner, are developing the thing, whatever it is,' put in Biggles grimly.

'Precisely,' interposed the Air Marshal dryly. 'I need hardly point out that if it goes on we soon shan't have any Air Force left in this part of the world. We're relying on you to get to the bottom of it.'

Biggles looked startled. 'But if your technical experts have failed, sir, what do you think I can do about it?'

The Air Marshal shrugged. 'I haven't the remotest idea. We're floored, stumped. Do what you can.'

'But that's all very well, sir,' protested Biggles. 'As far as I can see, to send my pilots out looking for nobody-knows-what, would merely be to send them for a Burton* to no useful purpose.'

'You're our last hope, Bigglesworth,' said the Air Commodore, with something like despair in his voice. 'We can't just suspend air operations—we might as well pack up altogether as do that.'

'If you go on losing pilots and machines at the rate you are evidently losing them it will come to the same thing in the end.'

The Air Marshal stepped in again. 'See what you can do, Bigglesworth. You can have *carte blanche*, a freelance commission, have what equipment you like, do what you like, go where you like—*but this thing has got to be stopped*.'

Biggles tapped a cigarette on the back of his hand. 'Very well, sir. I don't mind going out myself, but it isn't going to be very nice to have to ask my boys to virtually commit suicide. They'll go if I tell them to *go*, but I'd like you to know how I feel about it. This business of watching one's officers go one by one—'

'That's just how four other station commanders are feeling at this very moment, Bigglesworth,' broke in the Air Commodore wearily.

Biggles pulled forward a scribbling-pad and picked up a pencil. For a little while he made meaningless marks. Then he asked: 'What about altitude? Does that make any difference?'

'None,' answered the Air Commodore. 'In desperation we tried sending machines to their ceiling before

* Slang: to be killed.

20

leaving the airfield. They disappeared just the same.'

'I see. What is the longest period you have maintained radio contact with an aircraft that subsequently disappeared?'

'Four hours. That was on the Chungking run. It's a thousand miles.'

'No intermediate landing-ground?'

'None.'

'And what is the shortest period before you lost touch with a machine?'

'An hour.'

Biggles shrugged. 'The thing becomes uncanny. The time interval between one and four hours, translated to distance, is six or seven hundred miles. How can one even start looking for a thing that can strike over such an enormous area? You say that all the machines which disappeared, vanished into the blue. Am I to understand that not one of these crashes has ever been found?'

'That, unfortunately, is so,' answered the Air Commodore. 'You've flown over the Himalayas, and the Burmese jungle, so you know what it's like. It would be easier to find a pin in a cornfield.'

'These crashes, then, always occur over enemy-occupied country?'

'Either that or over the sea. From here we operate over Burma. From Madras and Ceylon most of the flying is done over the Indian Ocean.'

'There has never been an unexplainable crash in India itself?'

'There have been one or two crashes—not more than one would expect in the ordinary course of flying routine. These crashes were, of course, examined—but you know what such a crash looks like?'

'No unusual features emerged at the courts of inquiry?'

'None. In each case the pilot was killed, so he couldn't tell us anything, even if there was something to tell. There was a crash on this aerodrome two days ago. The pilot tried hard to say something before he died—but there, that could happen anyway.'

'Had he been over enemy territory?'

'Yes.'

'What about the machine?'

'There was nothing wrong with it, as far as could be ascertained.'

'How long had this pilot been in the air?'

'About twenty minutes. He left a formation and turned back.'

'Why?'

'We don't know. There was nothing very remarkable about that. Machines occasionally turn back for one reason or another.'

'What I'm trying to get at is this,' explained Biggles. 'Has there ever been an instance of an aircraft, or a pilot, affected by the new weapon, crashing on our side of the lines?'

'Not as far as we know—unless the pilot I just mentioned was a case. That seems most unlikely though, as he was one of a formation of ten. Had he been attacked, surely the others would have been attacked, too.'

'Tell me about this particular show,' invited Biggles.

'It was the last big raid we attempted from this airfield,' replied the Air Commodore. 'The rot had already set in, you understand, so the pilots and air crews taking part were keyed up for trouble. Actually, there are four squadrons here, not counting yours; two bomber squadrons and two fighter. Incidentally, you have been posted here as a communication squadron. Two days ago, one of the bomber squadrons took off

soon after dawn with every machine it could raise—
ten Blenheims—for a raid on the enemy-occupied airfield at Akyab. The distance to the objective, by the
direct route across the Bay of Bengal, is about four
hundred miles. Actually, the raid was timed for dawn,
but there was still some mist about so the take off was
postponed till it cleared.'

'And you say the pilots were aware of the mysterious
weapon?'

'Yes. All personnel were very much on the alert.'

'Go on, sir.'

'About twenty minutes after the take-off one of the
Blenheims was seen coming back. It was fairly low,
gliding, in a manner which might be described as
unsteady.'

'Which implies that the pilot was having trouble?'

'Yes—but then, had he not been in trouble he would
not have left the formation.'

'Did he speak over the radio?'

'No.'

'So you have no idea what the trouble was?'

'Not the remotest. Shortly after passing over the
boundary of the airfield the aircraft stalled, and
crashed, with what result I have already told you. At
the Court of Inquiry, which went into the evidence
very carefully, it was decided that such an accident
could occur quite apart from any secret weapon. In
fact, it was that sort of accident that could occur, and
does occur, regularly.'

'What was the name of this pilot?'

'Cratton.'

Biggles made a note. 'What happened to the rest of
the formation?'

'The flight ended in disaster,' said the Air Commodore heavily. 'An hour after taking off, one of the nine

remaining machines, before enemy opposition was encountered, without warning went into a spin and fell into the sea. Just before reaching the objective, in precisely the same conditions, another machine went down. One was shot down in combat over the target area. The six survivors dropped their bombs and turned for home. On the return journey four more went down at irregular intervals. Only two got back safely, both perfectly all right beyond being shaken by the tragedy of their comrades, and the strain of flying with the same fate impending.'

'There was absolutely nothing wrong with them physically?'

'Nothing.'

'And what about the machines?'

'They were all right, too.'

'And the surviving pilots could offer no explanation as to why the others went down?'

'None. The story was the same in every case. The stricken machine flew badly for a moment or two and then appeared to fall out of control. Sometimes the engines were cut, sometimes, the machines hit the water with the motors running.'

Biggles lit a fresh cigarette. 'I understand what you mean about pilots becoming unnerved. Anyone would freeze to the stick with that sort of thing going on round him. As far as a solution to the mystery is concerned, inevitably one thinks of death rays, so called, which I believe have often been used in fiction, but never in fact. Scientists say that such a ray is not possible—but then, scientists are not always right.'

'You think there may be something in the death ray idea, then?' suggested the Air Marshal. 'We've considered it, of course.'

'Frankly, no,' replied Biggles. 'And I'll tell you why.

24

If such a device was being used one would suppose that once they were within the sphere of influence all machines would be affected. In a daylight raid most aircraft keep a tight formation. I mean, if the thing could strike down one machine surely it would be able to strike down the others? We can hardly suppose that some machines are vulnerable while others are not. How was it that two came back? They were in all respects identical with those that fell. Then again, why the interval of time between the falling out of the last machines?'

The Air Marshal spoke. 'Our experts assert positively that the death ray is not yet a practical proposition, but there may be a beam device which could affect the electrical installation of an aero engine. For want of any other explanation we are inclined to accept that view.'

'I'm not,' returned Biggles bluntly.

'Why not?'

'In the first place, because the failure of its power unit doesn't necessarily cause an aircraft to go down out of control. The pilot would automatically put the machine into a glide, and while the machine was gliding he would have ample time to send out a signal. Then again, air crews wear parachutes. If the aircraft was vitally affected the men in it would bale out. To me it looks more as if machines are being sabotaged on the ground.'

'You can rule out sabotage,' said the Air Commodore. 'Those Blenheims were inspected and tested down to the last detail before they left the ground. With all this going on you can be quite sure that close watch is kept on equipment.'

Biggles thought for a moment. 'The one incontestable fact is that something is going wrong. If the trouble isn't caused in the air, then it must start on the ground. Against trouble in the air is the absence of anything like structural failure, which would certainly be spotted by the other machines in the formation. I still think it is extraordinary that none of these crews baled out, or tried to bale out.'

'It isn't always easy to abandon an aircraft that is falling out of control,' remarked the Air Commodore.

'And in the case of Blenheims the Bay of Bengal was underneath, don't forget,' put in the Air Marshal. 'The bay is infested with sharks.'

'That may have been the reason,' agreed Biggles. 'For all we know, the crews of some of the machines that were lost on the China route *may* have baled out. Even if they got down alive, I imagine they'd find it impossible to get back on foot.'

There was another short silence. All eyes were on Biggles' face as he pondered the problem.

'Tell me,' he went on presently, 'was there any rule about the number of pilots in these lost machines? I mean, has disaster ever overtaken a machine with two pilots in the cabin?'

The Air Commodore answered. 'I'm not quite sure about that. Out here we have to be economical with pilots, so in most cases—it was on the China run—when two pilots were lost together.'

Again silence fell. Biggles chewed a matchstalk reflectively. Outside, the brief tropic twilight was passing, but the sultry heat persisted. The Air Commodore switched on a light. A large white moth flew in through the open window and fluttered round the globe with a faint rustling sound as its wings beat with futile effort against the glass.

'Any more questions, Bigglesworth?' asked the Air Marshal anxiously.

26

Biggles looked up. 'No, sir.' He smiled wanly. 'You've given me plenty to think about. I'd like to sleep on it.'

'Then you'll—er—take the matter in hand?'

'I'll do my best with it, sir.'

'It's urgent—desperately urgent.'

'That's about the only aspect of this affair that's really obvious, sir,' answered Biggles. He got up. 'I'll go now and have a word with my officers. Between us we may get on the scent of the thing. If we do I'll report to the Air Commodore. I take it that no one on the station will be told the real reason why we have come here?'

'I'll see to that,' promised the Air Commodore. 'Even the station commander, Group Captain Boyle, supposes you to be an ordinary communication squadron, sent out here for special duty.'

'He's not likely to interfere with us?'

'No. I've told him that you will come directly under the Higher Command for orders. The presence here of the A.O.C. will confirm that.'

'Very good, sir. By the way, are you staying on here?'

'For the time being, at any rate,' answered Air Commodore Raymond. 'You can regard me as a sort of liaison officer between you and the Air Officer Commanding. Call on me for anything you need.'

Biggles saluted and withdrew. Deep in thought, and not a little worried, he made his way along the silent tarmac to the quarters that had been allocated to the squadron.

Chapter 3
Biggles Briefs Himself

The buzz of conversation died abruptly as Biggles walked into the ante-room and closed the door behind him. Only the radio went on, unheeded, relaying swing music from London. A short, stoutish, olive-skinned, middle-aged man, dressed in white duck trousers and mess-jacket, wearing a beaming smile, was standing by a low table on which rested a brass tray bearing a coffee-pot and cups.

Biggles called to him. 'Hi!, you; that'll do,' he said curtly.

'Plenty coffee, sahib. You like some, mebbe?' answered the steward.

'When I want anything I'll let you know,' returned Biggles. 'Pack up now.'

'Velly good, sahib.' Still beaming, the steward picked up his tray and departed.

Biggles looked at Algy. 'Who's that?'

'Lal Din.'

'Who's he?'

'One of the waiters from the canteen. He's all right.'

'I don't doubt it,' replied Biggles. 'But it's better not to talk in front of staff. They gossip.' He indicated the radio with a thumb. 'Turn that thing off, somebody.'

Angus complied.

'What's cooking, chief?' asked Tex eagerly.

'A dish with a nasty smell and a worse flavour,' replied Biggles quietly. 'Gather round, everybody, and I'll tell you about it. By the way, has anybody been out on the station?'

Several voices answered. 'I had a look round to see what machines we had on charge,' said Algy. 'Some of the others took a stroll to get their bearings.'

'In that case you may have heard something?' suggested Biggles.

'I didn't hear anything, but there's a sort of grey atmosphere in the central mess,' put in Ginger. 'There were only a few chaps there, but they looked at me as if I were something blown in off a dunghill.'

'I ran into Johnny Crisp on the perim*,' said Algy. 'You remember him—he picked up two bars to his D.F.C. in Wilks' squadron? He's a flight-loot** in 818 Squadron now. He told me a little. Ginger is right about the atmosphere. It's sort of—brittle, as if everyone was waiting for an unexploded bomb to go off. Johnny has aged ten years since I last saw him, a few months ago.'

Biggles nodded. 'I'm not surprised. I'll tell you why.'

He devoted the next twenty minutes to a résumé of the sinister story he had just gathered at headquarters. No one interrupted. All eyes were on his face. When he concluded, still no one spoke.

'Well, has nobody anything to say?' queried Biggles.

'What is there to say?' asked Ginger.

'Sure, I guess you're right, at that,' put in Tex, blowing a cloud of cigarette smoke at the ceiling. 'Looks like we've come a helluva long way to find trouble. So what?'

'Has anybody an idea about this thing?' demanded Biggles.

No one answered.

---

* Slang: perimeter
** Slang: Flight Lieutenant

'Stiffen the crows!' exclaimed Biggles. 'You are a bright lot. Do I have to do all the thinking?'

'What's the use of us trying to work it out if you can't?' murmured Tug.

'What do you think about it yourself, old boy?' asked Bertie.

'Frankly, I can't even begin to think,' admitted Biggles. 'We have one single fact to work on. Something is affecting our machines, or the pilots. We don't even know which. That's the first thing we've got to find out.'

'You tell us how, and we'll get right on with it,' asserted Ferocity.

'That would be easier if I knew what we were looking for,' went on Biggles. 'One thing is certain. We shan't find it by sitting here. We've got to go out—where the others went. That will mean . . . casualties. And that's putting it nicely. We aren't the only suicide squadron on the station, but that doesn't make it any easier from my point of view. I've never yet asked a man to do a show I wouldn't do myself, so I shall make a start. After that it will be a job for volunteers. If anyone would like to fall out, he may. Now's the time.'

Nobody moved.

Biggles glanced round. 'Okay, if that's how you feel about it,' he said softly. 'Now you know what's likely to happen, let's get down to it. I shall make a start in the morning by going up to Jangpur, the Indian terminus of the China run, to have a look round. I am planning to take an aircraft over the course.'

'You mean—go to Chungking?' cried Algy.

'Yes.'

'But that's daft, mon,' protested Angus. 'How can ye find a thing when ye dinna ken what ye're looking for?'

'Has anyone an alternative suggestion?'

There was a chorus of voices offering to go out, but Biggles silenced them with a gesture. 'Don't all talk at once, and don't let's have any argument about who is going out. You'll all get your turns. I shall do the first show. That's settled. If I don't come back Algy will take over. If he fades out, too, the others will carry on in order of seniority until the thing is found, or until there is no one left to look for it. That's all quite simple. What machines have we got, Algy?'

'A mixed bunch,' was the reply. 'It looks as if Raymond has got together anything he thought might be useful. There's a Wimpey, a Beaufighter, a Mosquito, three Hurricanes, three Spits* and a Typhoon. If you've made up your mind to go out why not take the Beau, and have somebody else with you? Then, if anything went wrong, the second pilot could bring the aircraft home.'

'From what I understand, flying two pilots together is just an easy way of doubling the rate of casualties. Two go instead of one. Whether the new weapon affects the men or the machine, the whole outfit goes west.'

'That doesn't entirely fit in with what Johnny Crisp told me,' declared Algy.

'What did he tell you?'

'Well, it seems that some fellows are either extraordinarily lucky, or else they—or their machines— are unaffected by the new weapon.'

'What do you mean by that, precisely?'

'Johnny tells me that he has made eleven sorties since the trouble started and has never seen or heard anything to alarm him. But he has seen others go down, seen them dropping like shot birds all round him—

* Spitfire fighter

that's how he put it. He told me that what with this ropey spectacle, and expecting his own turn to come every minute, he froze to the stick, with fright. Once he was the only one of five to return. Another chap, a pilot officer named Scrimshaw, has been out nine times, and has got away with it.'

Biggles regarded Algy with a mystified look in his eyes. 'That certainly is interesting,' he said slowly. 'What squadrons are these chaps in?'

'They're both in 818, flying Hurrybombers*. There are only five of them left in the squadron, although they have had replacements several times. Some chaps went west on their first show.'

'I suppose it must be luck, but it seems strange,' muttered Biggles. 'There can't be anything unusual about their machines—they're all standardised.'

'They haven't always flown the same machines, anyway,' volunteered Algy.

'Then obviously we can't put their luck down to their equipment. Yet the fellows themselves must be flesh and blood, like any other men. It *must* be luck. I don't see how it can be anything else.'

'If this new weapon is so hot, why haven't the Japs handed it on to their partners, the Nazis?' inquired Henry Harcourt.

'Ask me something easier,' returned Biggles. 'All the same, Henry, I think you've got something there. So far the trouble is localised in the East. One would suppose that the Japs would pass it on to the Nazis. All I can say is, God help us if they do.'

'Maybe the Japs don't trust the Nazis,' contributed Ferocity, practically. 'They may be windy of having the thing turned on then, if ever they fell out with their

---

* Hurricane fighters modified to carry bombs under the wings.

partners.'

'That may be the answer,' acknowledged Biggles.

'How about gas?' suggested Henry. 'Have you thought of that?'

'It passed through my mind,' averred Biggles. 'But there are several arguments against it. The first is, you can only get gas in quantity to a great height, by carrying it, or shooting it up, and nobody has seen any sort of vehicle or missile capable of doing that. Then again, what about formations? If a trail of gas *could* be laid across the sky, why are some pilots affected and not others? And how are we going to account for the irregular intervals of time between the machines falling out? I can't believe that the Japs could plant gas all over the place, at different altitudes, without being spotted. Finally, if gas were used, what is there to prevent the Japs themselves from flying into it, bearing in mind that the locality would not be constant? The wind, upcurrents and sinkers, would blow the stuff all over the place. Still, we'll bear the possibility in mind.'

'It was just an idea,' murmured Henry.

'Let's get back to the question of action,' suggested Biggles. 'We've got to find this hidden horror before we can do anything about it, and no doubt some of us will do that. Plenty of others have found it,' he added significantly, 'but unfortunately they couldn't get the information home. In other words, without mincing matters, it seems that the man who finds the thing, dies. Our problem is to find it and live—or live long enough to pass back the secret. It means going out, and I shall make a start, beginning in the area where the thing struck first—that is, on the Jangpur-Chungking route. The rest of you will stay here till I get back. That's an order. On no account will anyone go into the air; nor will anyone refer to the fact, either here or anywhere else, that we have been sent out specially to hunt this thing down. At all times you will pretend that we are what we are supposed to be, a communication squadron scheduled for co-operation with forces inside India. You needn't be idle. Give the machines a thorough overhaul. I shall go up to Jangpur in the Typhoon. Algy, I'd like you to get a list of all persons outside Air Force personnel who work on the station, or have permits to visit the airfield for any purpose whatsoever. There are certain to be a lot of men of the country; there always are on Indian stations. For the benefit of those of you who haven't been to India before, we don't use the expression *natives*. It's discourteous. Raymond probably has such a list already made. That would be the first thing he'd do, I imagine, in checking up for possible saboteurs. If anyone asks where I've gone you can say I'm doing a test flight—which will be true enough. Now let's get some sleep.'

Chapter 4
Biggles Makes a Wager

The following morning, the first glow of dawn saw Biggles in the air, in the Typhoon, heading north for Jangpur, the Indian terminus of the China route. He had not far to go—a trifle more than a hundred miles. As he landed and taxied to the wooden office buildings he noted a general absence of movement, an atmosphere of inactivity. The duty officer, a pilot officer, came to meet him. His manner was respectful, but listless, as if his interest in everything about him was perfunctory. He told Biggles that the station commander, Squadron Leader Frayle, was in his office.

And there Biggles found him, looking as though he had not been to bed for a week. His eyes were heavy from want of sleep; his hair was untidy and his chin unshaven. The desk was a litter of dirty cups, plates and glasses.

Biggles did not appear to notice this. 'Good morning,' he greeted cheerfully. 'My name's Bigglesworth.'

The squadron leader's eyes brightened. 'So you're Biggles? I've heard of you. Take a seat. Can I get you anything?'

'No, thanks,' answered Biggles. 'At this hour of the morning I work better on an empty stomach.' He pulled up a chair and lit a cigarette.

'What in the name of all that's unholy brought you to this God-forsaken, sun-blistered dustbin?' inquired Frayle curiously.

'I'm told you've had a spot of trouble here,' replied

Biggles. 'I've been sent out from home to try to iron it out.'

'Go ahead,' invited Frayle bitterly. 'The airfield's yours—and you're welcome to it. I've lost four officers and four machines in four days—the last four to go out, in fact. That should encourage you to keep your feet on something more solid than the floor of a fuse-lage. I've three officers left out of eighteen. Not bad going, eh?'

'I heard the position was pretty grey,' said Biggles sympathetically.

'Grey! It's blacker than a black-out.' Frayle's voice took on a quality of bitter resentment. 'Grey, they call it. It's hell, that's what it is. Can you imagine what it's been like for me, to sit here day after day sending out lads who I know I shall never see again?'

'I can imagine it,' answered Biggles quietly.

'There's another one going this morning,' went on Frayle. 'I didn't order him to go. Not me. I've finished picking the roster with a pin to decide who was to be the next man to die. He just told me was going. There's a load of medical stores urgently needed in Chungking. To-morrow I shall be down to two pilots.'

'You haven't tried doing the run yourself?'

'No. As I feel that would suit me fine. My orders are to stay on the carpet. They say my job is on the station. Well, to-morrow I'm going, anyway, orders or no orders. I can't stand any more of this.'

'It's no use talking that way, Frayle,' said Biggles softly. 'You know you can't do that.'

'But I—I—' Frayle seemed to choke. He buried his face in his hands.

'Here, take it easy,' said Biggles gently. 'I know how you feel, but it's no use letting the thing get you down like this. Get a grip on yourself. Can't you see that by cracking up you're only helping the enemy? What about this lad—has he gone off yet?'

'No, they're loading up the machine.'

'Good. Stop him.'

Frayle looked up. 'But this stuff is supposed to go through.'

'I know. Never mind. Stop him.'

'But what shall I tell headquarters?'

'You needn't tell them anything. I'll take the stuff.'

'*You'll* take it?'

'Yes.'

'You're out of your mind.'

Biggles smiled. 'You may be right, but I'll take this stuff to Chungking just the same. Send for the lad who was going. What's his name?'

'Bargent. He's a flying officer—a South African. You'll find him as amiable as a rhino that's been shot in the bottom with a charge of buckshot.'

'I'll have a word with him. You snatch a bath, treat your face to a razor blade, and have something to eat; you'll feel better. I'll fix things while you're doing it.'

Frayle gave the necessary order. Presently Bargent came.

'Now what's boiling?' he demanded in a hard voice.

'You're not doing this show,' said Biggles.

'And who says so?' questioned Bargent hotly.

'I say so,' replied Biggles evenly.

Bargent flung his cap on the floor, which was to Biggles a clear indication of the state of his nerves.

'And if you start throwing your weight about with me, my lad, I'll put you under close arrest,' promised Biggles, in a voice that made the flying officer stare at him.

'But I *want* to go, sir,' said Bargent, in a different tone of voice.

Biggles thought for a minute. 'All right. You can come with me if you like.'

'With you?'

'That's what I said.'

The South African laughed shortly. 'Okay. The machine is all ready.'

Biggles turned to Frayle. 'How many machines have you got left?'

'Two, able to do the run.'

'What are they?'

'Wimpeys.'

'And one's loaded?'

'Yes.'

'Did that arrangement appear in last night's orders?'

'Yes.'

'In the ordinary way the other machine would stand in a shed all day?'

'Yes.'

'Have you a duplicate set of these medical stores?'

'We've a hundred tons, all overdue for delivery.'

'Where are they?'

'In store.'

'Locked up?'

'Yes.'

'Who's your storekeeper?'

'Corporal Jones.'

'That's fine,' declared Biggles. 'I'm going to try being unorthodox. For a start we're going to unload this loaded machine, and take every package to pieces. Then we'll take the machine to pieces.'

'You're wasting your time.'

'What do you mean?' asked Biggles quickly.

'We've tried that a dozen times. You suspect sabotage? So did we. The first action I took was what you propose doing now, supposing that someone was

38

sticking a time bomb in the load. We've never found such a thing, or anything like it.'

Biggles thought for a little while. 'H'm. I was bound to try that,' he asserted. 'But if you've already done it there doesn't seem to be much point in repeating it, so we'll proceed with the second part of the programme. I want you to go and tell Corporal Jones, privately, to prepare a second load. Tell him to keep it out of sight. Swear him to secrecy. In a minute or two I'll bring the spare machine over and we'll load it ourselves.'

'What shall I do with the first load? The machine is waiting to go.'

'For the time being leave it just as it is. Put a guard over it.'

'This all seems a waste of time to me, but I'm willing to try anything,' said Frayle heavily.

'Then go and talk to Jones. Tell him to get a move on. Then I'd advise you to have a clean up. You may be sick, but it does no good to advertise it.'

Frayle went off.

Biggles turned to Bargent. 'You don't fancy your chance of coming back from this trip, do you?'

'Not much. Do you?'

'Yes. I think we've quite a good chance.'

'What leads you to think you are any different from anyone else?' Bargent couldn't keep sarcasm out of his voice.

'I didn't say I was different. But I've done quite a lot of flying, and I've never yet seen in the air anything capable of knocking a machine down without showing itself. I doubt very much if there is such a thing. So far, anything I've seen I've been able to dodge. It may sound like conceit, but I fancy my chance of going on doing that.'

'Would you like to bet on it?'

Biggles hesitated, but only for a moment. 'I don't go in much for betting, but I'd risk a hundred cigarettes.'

'I'll take that,' declared Bargent. 'Just what is the bet?'

'The bet is, by lunch-time I shall be in Chungking, and back again here for dinner to-night.'

'You hope,' muttered Bargent. 'I'd say you're on a loser.'

Biggles laughed. 'Well, you can't win, anyway.'

Bargent started. 'Why not?'

'If I lose—that is if we don't get back—I doubt if I shall be in a position to pay you and you'll be in no case to collect your winnings. We shall both be somewhere either on the mountains or in the jungle between here and China.'

'I'm nuts. I never thought of that,' said Bargent, grinning, and then laughing aloud.

'That's better,' remarked Biggles. 'While you can keep a sense of humour you've got a chance. Come on, let's go and get the Wimpey.'

Ignoring the machine that had been detailed, with its little crowd of loaders, they walked over to the hangar in which the spare machine was parked. Biggles climbed into the cockpit. 'You stay where you are,' he told Bargent. 'Walk beside me when I taxi over to the store. If anyone tries to get within ten yards of this machine throw something at him. If you let anyone touch you, my lad, you're not getting into this aircraft. I'm standing to lose more than a hundred cigarettes on this jaunt and I'm not taking any chances. Understand?'

'Okay.'

Biggles started the engines and taxied slowly through the glaring sunlight to the store shed. On the way, some of the porters that had been working on the other machine came hurrying across, but Bargent waved his arm, and yelled to them to keep away. He picked up and hurled a stone at one man who came on after the others had stopped. He retreated.

Frayle, in a bath wrap, appeared at the storehouse door.

'Is the stuff ready?' shouted Biggles.

'Yes, it's all here.'

'Help us to get it on board. Tell Jones to punch on the nose anybody who tries to get near us.'

'You do have some quaint ideas,' said Frayle, as he complied.

'Maybe that's why I'm here,' murmured Biggles.

In ten minutes the big machine was loaded to capacity with bundles of British and American stores, labelled CHUNGKING.

'What about something to eat before you go?' suggesting Frayle.

'No, thanks,' refused Biggles.

'It's a long trip.'

'We can manage.'

'Not even a last drink?' queried Bargent.

'Not even a last drink,' decided Biggles firmly. 'I make a point of doing one thing at a time, and the thing at the moment is to get this pantechnicon to China. Get aboard. So long, Frayle. I'm aiming to be back for tea.'

'I'll have it ready,' promised Frayle.

'Put a guard on my Typhoon. Don't let anyone touch it.'

'Okay.'

Before Bargent had properly settled himself in his seat Biggles had opened the throttle, and the big machine was bellowing across the airfield.

'Have you made this trip before?' asked Biggles, as

he throttled back to a steady cruising speed of just over two hundred miles an hour.

'Four times.'

'You must be lucky.'

'Maybe so. But I reckoned it couldn't go on. No sense in riding your luck too hard.'

'I suppose that's why you were trying it on again to-day?' said Biggles smoothly.

'Pah! It had to come sooner or later, and after seeing the others go, I thought the sooner the better.'

'Desperate fellow,' murmured Biggles. 'Well, we shall see. Keep your eyes skinned.'

'I suppose you realise that we're flying without gunners in the turrets?' said Bargent suddenly. 'That's asking for trouble, isn't it?'

'I have a feeling that we shan't need guns on this trip.'

'Why not?'

'Put it this way. Guns couldn't save the other crews. If guns can't stop this rot what point was there in bringing gunners? In the event of things going wrong we should only push up the casualty list. My gosh! That's pretty rough country below.' Biggles was looking below and ahead at a terrible yet magnificent panorama of mountain peaks that stretched across the course from horizon to horizon.

'It's like that pretty well all the way to China,' asserted Bargent. 'Where it isn't mountains, it's what the books call untamed primeval forest. Anyone going down in it wouldn't have a hope. They say it's unexplored.

'Let's hope we shan't have to explore it,' returned Biggles. 'Let me know if you see anything strange, in the air or on the ground.'

After that the two pilots fell silent. The Wellington

droned on, devouring space at a steady two hundred and twenty miles an hour. Mountains, groups and ranges and isolated peaks, many crowned with eternal snow, rolled away below. Valleys and depressions were choked with the sombre, everlasting forest.

'It's about time we were bumping into something,' said Bargent once, after looking at the watch. 'We must be half-way.'

'Begins to look as if this trip is going to cost you a hundred cigarettes, my lad,' said Biggles slyly, with a sidelong glance at his companion.

'If I don't lose more than that I shan't grumble,' murmured Bargent.

Two hours later the airport of Chungking came into view.

'That's it,' confirmed Bargent. 'What's the programme when we get there?'

'We'll sling this stuff overboard and start straight back,' replied Biggles.

'We're not stopping for lunch?'

'We're not stopping for anything.'

Bargent shook his head. 'You certainly are a strange bird,' he muttered.

'So I've been told. But never mind the compliments. As soon as we're in, jump down and keep the crowd away from this machine. I don't want anybody to touch it. I'll push the stuff out. They can collect it after we've gone. I shall leave the motors running.'

'Okay.'

As soon as the Wellington was on the ground a crowd of Chinese surged towards it; but Bargent held them off, gesticulating furiously. Biggles was throwing the stores out.

A Chinese officer came forward, speaking English.

'That's close enough!' shouted Bargent. 'Here's your

stuff. Some more will be coming through.'

'You in great hurry,' said the Chinaman impassively.

'We've got to get back,' answered Bargent.

'No want any petrol?'

Bargent looked at Biggles.

'No!' shouted Biggles. 'We've got enough to see us home.'

'You no stay to eat?' questioned the Chinaman.

'Not to-day, thanks,' returned Bargent. 'I've got a date with a girl in Calcutta, and she'll jilt me if I'm not back on time.'

The Chinaman grinned. 'Me savvy.'

'Okay, Bargent!' shouted Biggles. 'Get aboard. We're on our way.'

The South African picked his way through the pile of bales that Biggles had thrown out of the aircraft, closed the door and resumed his seat. The engines roared, and the machine swung round, scattering the crowd, to face the open field. In another minute it was in the air again, India bound.

'Get those cigarettes ready,' said Biggles.

Bargent laughed. 'I'll help you smoke 'em.'

'Oh, no, you won't,' declared Biggles. 'I reckon I shall have won 'em.'

There was no incident of any sort on the home run. There was no flak; no aircraft of any type, friend or foe, was sighted. As they glided in to land Bargent swore that he had never felt better in his life.

Frayle, in uniform, greeted them. 'So you got back?' he cried in a voice of wonder.

'If you think this is a ghost plane, try walking into one of the airscrews,' invited Biggles. 'You'll find it hard enough, I'll warrant.'

'Well, that's a mystery,' said Frayle.

'Not quite so much of a mystery as it was,' returned

Biggles.

'What are you going to do now?'

Biggles glanced at the sun, now low in the west. 'I want to get back to Dum Dum before dark, but I've just time for a snack.'

'You think it's safe to use the route now?'

'I didn't say that,' answered Biggles quickly. 'The Chinese now have a little to go on with, so you can afford to keep everything on the ground till you hear from me again. Yes, I know we got away with it this time, but that trick may not work again. By changing the planes at the last minute we slipped a fast one on the enemy. More than that I can't tell you for the moment. I want you and Bargent to keep your mouths shut tight about this show. If you talk it may cost you your lives. Keep the machines grounded. I'll be back. Now let's go and eat.'

An hour later, in the crimson glow of the Eastern sunset, Biggles landed at Dum Dum and walked quickly to the mess, to be met by an enthusiastic squadron.

'I say, old boy, that's marvellous—absolutely marvellous,' declared Bertie. 'Don't tell me you've been to China?'

'There and back,' answered Biggles. 'Let's get inside. I've got to talk to you chaps, and I don't mind admitting that I'd rather curl quietly in a corner and go to sleep. I seem to have done a lot of flying lately.'

'If you're tired, why not leave it until to-morrow?' suggested Algy.

'Because to-morrow morning I shall be just as busy—and so, perhaps, will you.'

'The point is, did you spot the secret weapon?' demanded Ginger.

'Not a sign of it,' returned Biggles, with a ghost of a

smile. 'Serious, now, everybody. Lock the door, Ginger. To-day I carried out what we might call an experiment,' he went on, when everyone had settled down. 'It leads, as most experiments do, to another. To-morrow morning I'm going to do a sortie over Burma.'

'Alone?' queried Algy, looking askance.

'I hadn't thought of taking anyone,' admitted Biggles.

'At least take someone with you,' pressed Algy. 'There may be something in this double pilot idea.'

'It isn't that I'm trying to run the show single-handed,' asserted Biggles. 'It's just that I want to avoid casualties if it is possible. There's no point in using more men on a job than it calls for. One machine can do what I have in mind to-morrow morning. Why risk two?'

'Then why not take the Beau*, or the Mosquito, and have someone with you for company?' suggested Algy.

'Yes, I might do that,' agreed Biggles.

There was a chorus of voices offering to go, but Biggles held up a hand. 'There's only one way to settle this, and that's by drawing lots,' he declared. 'That doesn't apply to flight commanders, though; they'll get their turns if I don't come back. Algy, write six names on slips of paper and put them in a hat.'

'Aren't you going to tell us what happened to-day?' queried Tex, while Algy was doing this.

'There's really nothing to tell,' answered Biggles. 'Nothing happened: that's a fact.'

Algy came forward with a hat in which lay six slips of paper, folded.

'Shake 'em up,' ordered Biggles.

Algy shook the hat.

---

* Beaufighter—twin engine two-seater day and night fighter.

Biggles closed his eyes and put out a hand. His fingers closed over a slip. He raised it. In dead silence he unfolded it and glanced at the name. He took it to Tug and smiled.

'You're it, Tug,' he announced.

'Whoopee! That's a corker,' cried Tug. 'That's the first time I've ever won a draw in my life.'

'Unless it's your lucky day it's likely to be the last,' joked Biggles grimly.

'I'll risk it,' flashed Tug, grinning. 'What time do we leave the carpet?'

'We'll decide that when we see what the weather is like,' returned Biggles.

'Do we wear brollies*?'

Biggles shrugged. 'In this affair they don't seem to make much difference, but I suppose we might as well. Don't mention this sortie to a soul, neither in nor outside the mess. Should anyone ask what we are doing you can say we're browning off waiting for orders. That's all. Let's go in to dinner.'

* Slang: parachutes

47

Chapter 5
Suicide Patrol

It was still dark, but with that faint luminosity in the sky that heralds the approach of the Eastern dawn, when Biggles was awakened by the sudden bellow of an aero engine. This is not an unusual sound on an airfield, and he turned over with the intention of snatching a final nap, supposing that the noise was created by a motor under test. But when a second, and then a third engine opened up, he sprang out of bed and strode to the window. In the eerie light of the false dawn he could just discern the silhouettes of what he thought were Hurricanes, moving slowly on the far side of the airfield. For a moment or two he stood gazing, sleep banished, a frown puckering his forehead; then he slipped a dressing-gown over his pyjamas and picked up the telephone.

Two minutes later Algy arrived, also in pyjamas. 'What's going on?' he asked tersely.

Biggles hung up the receiver. 'Take a look outside,' he invited. 'Those five survivors of 818 Squadron are going off on a bomb raid in the danger area. My God! They've got a nerve.'

Algy nodded. 'Yes, I remember now. Johnny Crisp told me last night that there was some talk of a final do-or-bust show in the hope of finding the thing that killed the others.'

'They'll do that, no doubt—or some of them will,' returned Biggles, in a hard voice.

'Johnny said they were going crazy, just sitting on

the ground doing nothing. He, being the only remaining flight commander, will lead the sortie. Personally, I think he's right. You know how it is; when a fellow's nerves start slipping he has only one chance of saving himself—if he ever wants to fly again; and that's to get in the air.'

'Maybe. But these chaps are practically committing suicide, and they must know it.'

'Johnny, and the other fellow I told you about, Scrimshaw, have always got back,' reminded Algy.

'So far. But there's such a thing as pushing your luck too hard.' Biggles started. 'Just a minute! Yes, that's it. I'm going to hook on to this raid, to watch what happens. All the evidence we have up to now is hearsay.'

Algy's eyes opened wide. 'But—'

'Don't stand gibbering. Go and get Tug out of bed and tell him to meet me on the tarmac in five minutes.'

'What about breakfast?'

'There'll be more time for that when we get back.'

'You mean—*if* you get back,' said Algy, with gentle sarcasm. 'Okay.' He departed.

Five minutes later, when Biggles went outside, Tug was there, waiting, parachute slung over his shoulder. The rest of the squadron was there, too, grim-faced, silent. The five Hurricanes were just taking off, sending clouds of dust swirling across the parched airfield.

'Look at 'em,' said Biggles in a low voice. 'There they go. That's guts for you. Come on, Tug; we'll catch 'em in the Mosquito.' It did not seem to strike him that he was doing the same thing. He glanced round the ring of anxious faces, and smiled the strange little smile they all knew so well. 'So long, chaps; keep your tails up.'

'I say, old boy, watch out what you're up to, and all

that,' blurted Bertie.

'May I follow in a Spit?' cried Ginger huskily.

'No,' answered Biggles shortly.

'But—'

'You heard me. Come on, Tug. Let's get cracking, or we'll lose sight of those crazy Hurry-wallahs.'

In a few minutes the Mosquito, probably the best and fastest long-range medium bomber in the world, was in the air. It carried no bombs. Biggles was at the control column, with Tug sitting beside him instead of adopting the prone position which the special structure of this type of aircraft permits. Both wore the regulation parachutes. The five Hurricanes were mere specks in the fast-lightening sky, but the Mosquito began slowly to overhaul them.

Below, looking eastward, like an army of black snakes, was the pattern of waterways that comprise the delta of the river Ganges. Rivers, streams, and irrigation canals, lay asprawl a flat, monotonous terrain, cutting it into a vast archipelago before emptying themselves into the Bay of Bengal. Here and there a village nestled in a verdant bed of paddy-fields, or clung precariously to the fringe of one of the numerous masses of forest that had invaded the fertile land from the east. By the time these had given way to the more sombre green of the interminable Burmese jungle the sky was turning from lavender to blue, with the Mosquito about a mile astern and two thousand feet above the Hurricane formation.

'What's their objective—do you know?' queried Tug.

'Apparently there's a bridge over the Manipur River which the army is anxious to have pranged*, to interrupt the Jap lines of communication.'

---

* Slang: to bomb a target successfully.

'Do you know where it is?'

'Not exactly, but it's somewhere north-west of Mandalay; you'll find it on the map.'

Tug unfolded the map on his knees and studied it closely for a minute. 'Okay, I've got it,' he remarked.

'We must be pretty close to enemy country, even if we're not actually over it,' said Biggles presently. 'Let me know at once if you see anything suspicious. You might get down and have a squint below, to see if you can spot any sign of ground activity.'

Tug dropped to the prone position and for a little while subjected the landscape to a searching scrutiny. Then he climbed back to his seat. 'Not a blessed thing,' he stated. 'All I can see are trees and rivers. No sign of any trenches, or anything like that, to mark the no-man's-land between our troops and the Japs.'

'What with jungle and camouflage. I didn't expect to see much,' returned Biggles. His eyes were on the Hurricanes.

'Listen, Tug. We'd better have some sort of a plan. I'll watch the formation. You watch the sky. If you see anything, *anything*, let me know. Let me know, too, if you feel anything. If I see or feel anything unusual I'll let you know. It may sound silly, but if I start behaving in a manner that strikes you as odd, you take over and get back home straightaway.'

Tug grinned. 'Okay. Funny business, this waiting for something to go pop.'

'I don't think funny is the right word,' argued Biggles. 'I'd say it's dashed uncomfortable. We must be well over enemy country now, so something may happen any time. Hello—that tells us where we are.'

A few wisps of black smoke had appeared in the sky round the formation, which went on without altering course.

'That's ordinary flak*,' declared Tug.

Biggles had a good look at it before he answered. He even flew close to a patch, studied it suspiciously, and then dispersed it with his slipstream. 'I think you're right,' he agreed. 'Just ordinary flak.'

It soon died away and no more came up. A quarter of an hour passed without incident. The Hurricanes roared on with the Mosquito keeping its distance.

'I'll bet those boys are wondering what this Mossy is doing, trailing 'em,' chuckled Tug. 'They seem to be all right so far.'

'So do we.'

'Maybe it'll turn out to be a false alarm after all.'

'Maybe.' Biggles was noncommittal. Not for a moment did he take his eyes off the Hurricanes.

Another twenty minutes passed and the formation began to lose height, at the same time opening out a little.

'What are they doing?' asked Tug.

'It's all right. That bridge over the river ahead must be the target. They're going down to prang it. Keep your eyes skinned for enemy aircraft—or anything else.'

Nothing happened—that is, nothing out of normal routine. The Mosquito held its altitude, circling wide, while the fighter-bombers went down and did their work. Pillars of white smoke leapt skyward in the target area. Biggles noted one direct hit and two near misses, and made a note in the log he was keeping. There was no flak, no enemy opposition of any sort. The Hurricanes, their work done, turned away, closing in again to the original formation, and headed for home, taking some altitude.

---

* Exploding anti-aircraft shells.

'Well, that's that,' mused Biggles. 'I didn't see anything unusual, did you, Tug?'

'Not a thing,' muttered Tug. 'I don't get it.'

'One would have thought that if the Japs *could* have stopped them, they'd have done it on the way out, before the bombers reached their target,' said Biggles pensively. 'The thing gets more and more inexplicable. Keep a sharp look-out, we aren't home yet.'

'They're still flying pretty,' observed Tug after a glance at the Hurricanes.

'So are we if it comes to that,' answered Biggles, glancing at the watch on the instrument panel and making another note.

Fifteen minutes later he observed that one of the Hurricanes had moved slightly out of position, so that its opposite number had to swerve slightly to avoid collision. Biggles stiffened, staring, nerves tense, but aware that this might have been the result of a moment's carelessness on the part of the pilot. But when the same machine swerved, and began to sideslip, he uttered a warning cry.

'Look! There goes one of them!' he shouted. 'By heaven! Yes, he's going down!'

Tug did not answer. Both pilots watched while the Hurricane maintained its swerve, getting farther and farther away from the formation, which held on its course. At the same time the nose of the straying machine began to droop, until presently the aircraft was plunging earthward in a dive that became ever steeper.

'Pull out!' yelled Tug—uselessly. He began to mutter incoherently.

The Hurricane, still running on full throttle it seemed, roared on to a doom that was now only a matter of seconds.

'Why doesn't he bale out?' cried Tug in a strangled voice.

'No use, Tug. He's finished,' said Biggles through his teeth, and pushing the control column forward he tore down behind the stricken aircraft. A swift glance revealed the other four machines still in formation, but nose down, racing on the homeward course, which, in the circumstances, Biggles realised, was the wisest action they could take. Long before he could overtake the doomed aircraft it had crashed through the tree-tops and disappeared from sight like a stone dropping into opaque water.

Tug caught his breath at the moment of impact, and then cursed through bloodless lips. His face was pale and distorted with fury; his eyes glittered.

'No use swearing, Tug,' said Biggles evenly. 'That doesn't get anybody anywhere.'

He went on down and circled over the spot where the Hurricane had disappeared, revealed at short distance by fractured branches. Nothing could be seen. 'The crash hasn't taken fire, anyway,' he muttered, and then looked at his own instrument dials, in turn. 'We seem to be still okay,' he added. 'Do you feel all right, Tug?'

'More or less—just savage, that's all,' growled Tug.

'Keep watch up topsides,' warned Biggles.

Still circling, without taking his eyes from the scene of the tragedy he climbed back up to two thousand feet.

'Listen Tug,' he said crisply. 'I'm going to bale out.'

'You're *what*!'

'I'm going down.'

'What's the use? The chap in that kite hadn't a hope.'

'I know that, but I'm going down to try to find out

54

just what happened. Unless someone examines one of these crashes we may never know what causes them. This is my chance.'

'You'll get hung up in the trees.'

'That's a risk I shall have to take.'

'What about Japs? There may be some down there.'

'I've got a gun in my pocket.'

'But don't be crazy. How are you going to get home?'

'Walk, if necessary.'

'But we must be a hundred miles from the nearest of our troops. I can't pick you up. There ain't an open patch as big as a handkerchief within seeing distance.' Tug spoke in a shrill, protesting voice.

'All right, don't get excited,' returned Biggles. 'There is one way you can collect me, when I've seen what I want to see. Take a look at that river, about a mile away to the left.'

'What about it?'

'I don't know how deep it is, but if it has any depth at all it should be possible to put down a seaplane or flying-boat on it. Now listen carefully. After I bale out I want you to return to base, going full bore. Tell Algy what has happened. Tell him to find Raymond and get him to requisition a marine aircraft of some sort from anywhere he likes. I believe the Calcutta Flying Club used to have some Moth seaplanes—but I'll leave that to Raymond. Whatever he gets, you come back in it and pick me up. And when I say you I mean *you*. Algy will probably want to come, but he's in charge at base and my orders are on no account is he to leave. This is tricky country, and having seen the spot you should recognise it again. Is that clear so far?'

'Okay. Where do I pick you up, exactly?'

'I shall be waiting by the river, on this bank, as near as I can get to the larger of those two islands you can see. They stand in a straight reach of river so it ought to be all right for landing. That island is the mark. Take a good look at it before you go because they may be similar islands higher up or lower down the river.'

'Okay, skipper. Is there some way you can let me know if you get down all right?'

'I've got my petrol lighter. I'll make a smoke signal. If you see smoke you'll know I'm on the carpet. Take over now, and glide across the crash. There doesn't seem to be any wind to speak of.'

They changed places and Biggles opened the escape hatch.

Tug throttled back and began a run, at little more than stalling speed, towards the spot where the Hurricane had crashed.

'Keep her as she goes,' said Biggles. 'That's fine. See you later.' He disappeared into space.

Tug pushed the throttle open and having brought the aircraft to even keel banked slightly to get a view below. The parachute was floating down almost directly over the objective. He watched it sink lower and lower until eventually it remained stationary on the tree-tops.

'My God! He's caught up!' he muttered through dry lips. He continued to circle, watching, and saw the fabric split as a broken branch poked through it. But he could not see Biggles. He could only suppose that he was suspended by the shrouds somewhere between the tree-tops and the ground. It was several minutes before a thin column of smoke drifted up.

Tug drew a deep breath of relief, and blipped* his engines as a signal that the smoke had been seen. He

---

* To change the rhythm of the engines, by closing and opening the throttle.

turned to the river. For a minute he cruised up and down making mental pictures of the island from all angles. Then, banking steeply, he raced away on a westward course.

Chapter 6
Rendezvous With Death

Tug's fear that Biggles' parachute would become caught up in the tree-tops was fully justified; it would only have been remarkable had it been otherwise. Biggles knew this, so he was not surprised when he found himself swinging in his harness below tangled shrouds and torn fabric some thirty feet above the fern-carpeted floor of the jungle. He was not unduly alarmed, being well satisfied that he himself had escaped injury. By pulling on a line to increase his swing he managed without any great difficulty to reach a bough. In five minutes he had slipped out of his harness and made a cautious descent to the ground, leaving the parachute in the trees, where, he realised, it was likely to remain. A party of monkeys, after chattering at the intrusion, swung quietly away.

Perspiring profusely in the stagnant atmosphere from his exertions he mopped his face with his handkerchief, and after listening for a little while for sounds that might indicate danger, he made the smoke fire as arranged. His petrol lighter, an old letter from his pocket, and some sere undergrowth, provided the means. He heard Tug's answering signal, but he did not move until a fast-receding drone told him that the Mosquito was homeward bound. The sound died away and silence fell—a strange, oppressive silence, after the vibrant roar which had for so long filled his ears. Bracing himself for his ordeal, for he had no delusions about the harrowing nature of the task before him, he made his way to the crash. He had not far to go.

The Hurricane was much in the condition he expected. Both wings had been torn off at their roots. One hung from a splintered bough a short distance from the wreck; the other, fractured in the middle and bent at right angles, lay near the fuselage. The blades of the airscrew had folded up and the boss had bored deep into the soft leafmould. The fuselage was the right way up, more or less intact. The only sound was a soft drip-drip-drip, as liquid escaped from radiator, tank, or a broken petrol lead. Moistening his lips he walked on to the cockpit.

The pilot, whom he did not know, a lad of about twenty with flaxen hair and blue eyes, was still in his seat. He was dead. No attempt had been made to use the parachute. A head wound, where his forehead had come into contact with the instrument panel at the moment of impact, was alone sufficient to have caused death, which must have been instantaneous.

Biggles lifted the limp body out, laid it on the ground and removed the indentification disc. THOMAS GRAFTON MOORVEN, R.A.F., it read. He then took everything from the pockets—cigarette case, wallet, personal letters, some snapshots and some loose coins—and having made a little bundle of them in the handkerchief, put it on one side. This done, he paused again to mop his face, for the heat was stifling. It may have been the anger that surged through him, causing his fingers to tremble, that made the heat seem worse than it really was. Accustomed though he was to war, and death, there was something poignant about this particular tragedy that moved him strangely, making his eyes moist and bringing a lump into his throat. After months of training and eager anticipation the boy had travelled thousands of miles to meet his death without firing a shot. He had not even seen the enemy who had killed him, the weapon that had struck him down. Fully aware of the risks he was taking he had gone out willingly to seek the thing that had killed his comrades, only to meet the same fate, to die alone in the eternal solitude of a tropic forest. There would be no reward, no decoration for valour. Those at home would not even know how he died. This, thought Biggles, as he stood looking down on the waxen features, was not war. It was murder—and murder called for vengeance. His hand, he decided, would exact retribution, if the power were granted him. He drew a deep breath and set about the task for which he had descended.

First, he examined the body thoroughly, but could find no wound, no mark that might have caused death, apart from those that were obviously the direct result of the crash. There was no sign of burning, such as might have resulted from an electrical discharge of some sort. He examined the eyes closely, and noticed that the pupils were dilated. This struck him as unusual, but neither his technical nor medical knowledge could help him to associate it with a cause of death. He made a mental note of it, however.

He next turned to the aircraft, starting with the wings. He did not expect to find anything there, for had they in some mysterious way been fractured in the air he would have seen it before the machine crashed. They told him nothing, so he turned to the fuselage, beginning with the motor, paying particular attention to the ignition system. All electrical equipment seemed to be in perfect order. From airscrew to rudder he subjected the machine to such an inspection as he had never before devoted to any aircraft; yet for all his efforts he found nothing, no clue that might remotely suggest a solution to the mystery. Again mopping his face, and brushing away the mosquitoes that were attacking him, he returned to the cockpit. He had already been over it. He went over it again, methodically, but found nothing except normal equipment on both side, even smelt it. He was turning away when a small object on the floor, under the seat, caught his eye. He picked it up. It was a slip of paper, pink paper of the sort that is called greaseproof, about three inches square. There was printing on one side: WITH THE COMPLIMENTS OF CHARNEYS, LTD., LONDON. NOT FOR SALE. SUPPLIED FOR THE USE OF H.M. FORCES ONLY. He raised the paper to his nostrils. It smelt faintly of mint. Smiling wanly he screwed the paper into a ball, tossed it aside and resumed his search.

Finally, reluctantly, he gave up, no wiser than when he began. There was nothing more he could do, he decided. Tug might return at any time now, so he had better be making his way towards the river.

One last problem, one that had been in the background of his mind all along, now demanded solution. The aircraft, of course, would have to be burnt, to prevent it from falling into the hands of the enemy. But what about the body? He had no implement with which to dig a grave. There seemed little point in carrying it to the river, even if this were possible. The undergrowth was so thick that he alone, with both hands free, would find the operation difficult enough. Even if he succeeded in carrying the body to the river there would be the question of transport to the base. In any case it would involve prodigious labour and delay, which would jeopardise his life, and Tug's, for no reason outside sentiment. On the other hand he did not like the idea of leaving the body there to become the prey of creatures of the forest. He could think of only one method of disposing of it, and that was the way chosen by some of the greatest warriors of the past, the way of the Romans, the Vikings, the Indians. All reduced the bodies of their chiefs and warriors to ashes, burning their weapons, their warhorses, and their hounds with them. After all, many good airmen, including some of his best friends, had gone out that way, he reflected.

Having steeled himself for this last grim ceremony, he was moving forward when voices at no great distance brought him to an abrupt halt, in a listening attitude. There was no doubt about the voices; with them came a trampling and crashing of undergrowth. Very soon it was clear that those responsible for the disturbance were approaching.

Biggles drew back and found a perfect retreat among the giant fronds of a tree-fern. In doing this he was actuated by more than casual curiosity. It seemed possible, indeed it seemed likely, that the Hurricane had been seen to fall, in which case enemy troops would be sent out to locate it. There was just a chance that these men were part of the team that operated the secret weapon. If that were so they would be worth capturing for interrogation.

The voices and the crashing drew nearer. The men seemed to be in a carefree mood. Biggles could not speak a word of Japanese, but he was in no doubt as to the nationality of the newcomers. He took out his automatic, examined it, and waited. The voices continued to approach.

In a few minutes a man burst from the undergrowth. He stopped when he saw the crash, and then let out a shrill cry. A second man joined him.

Biggles was disappointed. They were ordinary Japanese soldiers, infrantrymen, dirty, with the usual twigs attached to their uniforms for camouflage purposes.Both carried rifles and were smoking cigarettes.

No other sounds came from the forest so it was fairly certain that they were alone.

Their immediate reaction to the spectacle before them was not unnatural. They broke into an excited conversation as they walked on to the fuselage. When one of them pointed at the dead pilot and burst out laughing, after a momentary look of wonder Biggles frowned: friend or foe, to European eyes the sight was anything but funny. When one of them kicked the body every vestige of colour drained from his face. His lips came together in a hard line; his nostrils quivered. Still he did not move. But when one of the men, with what was evidently a remark intended to be jocular, bent down and inserted his cigarette between the dead pilot's lips, and then, shouting with laughter, stepped back to observe the effect. Biggles' pent-up anger could no longer be restrained.

'You scum,' he grated. The words were low, but distinct.

The two Japanese spun round as if a shot had been fired. They stared in goggle-eyed amazement, no longer laughing, but fearful, as though confronted by a ghost—the ghost of the body they had violated. Superstitious by nature, they may have believed that.

Biggles spoke again. 'You utter swine,' he breathed.

This spurred the Japanese to movement. With a curious cry one of them threw up his rifle. Biggles fired. The man twitched convulsively. Again Biggles' automatic roared. The man's legs crumpled under him; the rifle fell from his hands and he slumped, choking. The second man started to run. Quite dispassionately, without moving from his position, Biggles took deliberate aim and fired. The Jap pitched forward on his face, but crying loudly started to get up. Biggles walked forward and with calculated precision fired two more shots at point-blank range. His lips were drawn back, showing the teeth. 'You unspeakable thug,' he rasped. The man lay still.

As the echoes of the shots died away a hush fell, sullen, hot, heavy. The only sound was the hum of innumerable mosquitoes. For a few seconds, breathing heavily, the smoking pistol in his hand, Biggles stood gazing at the man he had shot. Then he walked quickly to the dead pilot, snatched the cigarettes from his lips and hurled it aside.

'Sorry about that, Tommy,' he said quietly. 'Sort of thing one doesn't expect,' he added, as if he were talking to himself.

Pocketing his pistol he picked up the body, placed it gently in the cockpit and closed the cover. Then, lighting a slip of paper he dropped it by a leaking petrol lead. Fire took hold, spreading rapidly. In a moment the forepart of the aircraft was wrapped in leaping flames.

As Biggles stepped back his eyes fell on the Japanese. 'We've no dogs, Tommy,' he murmured; 'These hellhounds are a poor substitute, but they'll have to do.' Having confirmed that both were dead he dragged the bodies across the tail unit, which had not yet been reached by the flames, afterwards backing away quickly, for the ammunition belts were exploding their charges and bullets were flying. Picking up the handkerchief containing the dead pilot's belongings he walked to the edge of the clearing. There he turned and stiffened to attention. His right hand came up to the salute.

'So long, Tommy,' he said quietly. 'Good hunting.' Then, without a backward glance he strode away through the jungle in the direction of the river.

Behind him, to the roll of exploding ammunition, the

smoke of the funeral pyre made a white column high against the blue of heaven. He realised that it might be seen by the enemy and bring them to the spot. He didn't care. He rather hoped it would. He was in the sort of mood when fighting would be a pleasure.

It took him the best part of an hour to reach the river, and he was dripping with sweat when the turgid water came into view. The only living things in sight were a small crocodile, lying on a mudflat, and a grey heron, perched on a dead limb overhanging the water. There was no sign of Tug. He was some distance above the island that he had chosen for the rendezvous, and it required another twenty minutes of labour, working along the river bank, to bring him in line with it. There was still no sign of Tug, so choosing the crest of a small escarpment for a seat, he lighted a cigarette and settled down to wait. There was nothing else to do. The mosquitoes were still with him. He brushed them away with a weary gesture and mopped his dripping face, which was still pale, and set in hard lines. The strain of the last two hours had been considerable.

He passed the next half-hour in silent meditation, pondering over the events of the morning, and the problem which they had done nothing to elucidate, before he heard the sound for which he was waiting— the drone of an aircraft. But because his ears were attuned to the nicer distinctions between aero engines, at first he was puzzled. Very soon, though, he solved the mystery. There were two engines, of different types. The main background of sound was provided by the deep roar of a high-performance motor, but against it, quite distinct, there was the busy chatter of a lighter type. It seemed unlikely that there could be two light planes in that particular theatre of war, so he was not surprised when a Gipsy Moth float-plane swung into view, tearing low up the river. Behind it, weaving in wide zigzags but definitely keeping it company, was a Hurricane.

Biggles smiled faintly as he stood up and waved. The ill-assorted pair needed no explanation. Tug had returned in a marine craft as arranged, and it had brought an escort. Biggles' immediate reaction was one of relief, not so much on his own account as because, in spite of the secret weapon, Tug had obviously managed to get home, and make the return trip. He had been gone a long time, and Biggles had just begun to fear that the nameless peril had claimed him.

Tug evidently saw him at once, for he cut his engine and put the machine straight down on the water. Without waiting for it to finish its run he came round in a swirl of creamy foam to that point of the river bank where Biggles was now waiting. Biggles waded out through two feet of water and six inches of mud to the aircraft, and climbed aboard.

'Good work, Tug,' he greeted. 'have any trouble?'

Tug grinned. 'Not a trace. I saw a bunch of Zeros*, high up, as I went home, but they didn't see me. Did you find anything?'

'No.'

'Who was it—Grainger, Larkin, or Moorven?'

Biggles started. 'What do you mean?'

'All three failed to get back. The others say the hoodoo got 'em all.'

'The others? Do you mean that Johnny Crisp and Scrimshaw got back *again*?'

'They did. I left Johnny stamping and cursing on the airfield, and Scrimshaw roaring round in circles looking for somebody to shoot. Odd, ain't it?'

---

* Japanese fighter aircraft.

During this brief recital Biggles had remained still, half in and half out of the spare seat, staring at Tug's face. 'Odd! It's more than that. It's more than that. It's uncanny. It can't be luck. It *can't* be. But we'll talk about that when we get home. Who's in the Hurricane?'

'Angus.'

'Who told him he could come?'

'Algy.'

'Algy, eh? I like his nerve.'

Tug grinned again. 'Algy's in charge, don't forget, during your absence. Don't blame him. The whole bunch wanted to come and Algy had his work cut out to keep them on the carpet. They reckoned someone ought to come to keep an eye on me while I was keeping an eye open for you. In the end Algy agreed to let one of the flight commanders go. Angus and Bertie tossed for it. Bertie lost. I left him trying to rub a hole through his eyeglass.' While Tug had been speaking he had eased the throttle open a trifle and moved slowly to deeper water.

Biggles was looking up at the Hurricane. 'What the . . . ! What in thunder does Angus think he's doing?' he asked sharply.

Tug looked up and saw the fighter coming down in a shallow swerving dive as if it intended pancaking on the river. 'He's giving you the salute,' he said, slowly, in a voice that did not carry conviction.

Biggles did not answer at once. He stared, while the Hurricane continued its downward swoop. 'You're wrong,' he forced through dry lips. 'Angus has bought it. Look out!'

The warning was no mere figure of speech, for the Hurricane was coming in dead in line with the Moth. Tug realised it, and shoved the throttle open with a lightning movement of his hand. 'Hang on!' he yelled, as the engine roared and the light plane shot forward. He was only just in time.

The Hurricane's port wing-tip missed the Moth by inches. It struck the water with a mighty splash that drenched the Moth with spray and set it rocking violently. It bounced and splashed again, this time to disappear except for a swinging rudder.

Tug tore to the spot. 'I told him not to come!' he cried wildly. Then again, 'I told him not to come. I told him—'

'Shut up,' snapped Biggles. 'Watch for me,' he added, and dived overboard.

When, a minute later, he reappeared, gasping, with Angus in his arms, Tug was out on a float, on his knees, waiting. He took Angus first, and then helped Biggles to get astride the float. The weight tipped the plane at a dangerous angle, and Tug leaned away to the other float to counteract the list. Angus was dead or unconscious—it was not clear which.

'Help me to get him into the spare seat,' ordered Biggles.

'How is he do you think?'

'I don't know, but he must be in a bad way. He's got a broken leg, if nothing worse. We can't do anything for him here. His only chance, if he is still alive, is hospital.'

'But this machine won't lift three—there's no room, anyway.'

'I know it,' answered Biggles curtly. 'You get him back. I'll wait. I shall be all right here. You ought to be back in a couple of hours if nothing goes wrong. Better 'phone Algy from the slipway to let him know what's happened—and tell him to keep everybody on the ground till I get back. That's an order.'

'Okay,' grunted Tug.

After some delay, and with no small difficulty, Angus' limp body was lifted into the spare seat. As Biggles had said, there was no question of doing anything for him on the spot.

'Run me close to the bank and I'll get off,' said Biggles. 'There are crocs in this river.'

Tug taxied close to the bank and Biggles waded ashore.

'Okay – get cracking,' ordered Biggles.

Tug waved. The engine roared. The little plane swung round and raced away down the river. Biggles watched it until it was out of sight and then resumed his seat on the escarpment. Automatically he felt for his cigarette case. The cigarettes were, of course, soaking wet, so very carefully he laid them out on the rock to dry.

Chapter 7
Biggles Investigates

Biggles waited, waited while the sun climbed over its zenith and began its downward journey. In the low ground through which the river wound its sluggish course, the air, heavy with the stench of rotting vegetation, was still. The heat was suffocating. The swampy banks of the river steamed, the slime at the water's edge erupting gaseous bubbles. Biggles sweated. Once, a flight of three Mitsubishi bombers droned overhead on a westerly course; a little later six Zero fighters, flying at a great height, passed over, heading in the same direction, towards India.

'They must know our machines are grounded, so they're getting cocky,' mused Biggles.

It was clear that if the secret weapon was still in operation the enemy planes were not affected, which proved that the thing was under control, and discounted anything in the nature of poison gas which, once released, would be uncontrollable, and would— unless the Japanese pilots wore respirators—affect both friend and foe alike. If a beam, or ray, were being used, it could not be a permanent installation, for this also would operate against all types of aircraft regardless of nationality. Had enemy planes been insulated against such a ray the insulating material would have been discovered by technicians whose work it was to examine the enemy aircraft brought down on the British side of the lines. Not the least puzzling aspect of the new weapon was the distance over which it was effective—

or so it would seem from the immense area in which British machines had been brought down. It suggested that the instrument was highly mobile, or else there was a number of them installed at points throughout the entire forest. Yet if this were so, why had the Hurricanes been allowed to reach their objective? Had it been possible to stop them, then they would most certainly have been stopped. The fact that the Hurricane formation had reached its objective that morning suggested that the weapon had its limitations. Thus mused Biggles, sweltering on his lonely rock.

It was getting on for three hours before Tug returned. Biggles was glad to see the Moth, for apart from the delay, and the wearisome nature of his vigil, the danger of flying in the area had been demonstrated.

'You've been a long time,' greeted Biggles.

'I had to snoop around a bit,' answered Tug. 'There are bandits* about, poking their noses close to India— taking advantage of our machines being grounded, I suppose.'

'How's Angus?' asked Biggles anxiously, as he climbed aboard.

'He's alive, but that's about all. They took him to hospital. I didn't wait for details.'

'Did he recover consciousness?'

'No.'

'You spoke to Algy?'

'Yes. I 'phoned him.'

'What did he say?'

'Oh, he got a bit worked up—wanted to send the gang out, for escort. I told him what you said about staying put. He just made noises.'

'Where did you get this Moth, by the way?'

* RAF code for enemy aeroplanes

'Raymond fixed it. It was up a backwater the other side of Calcutta. Raymond lent me his car to get to it. It used to belong to an air taxi company. That's all I know. It flies all right—and that's all I care.'

'As we can't land at Dum Dum we shall have to go back to the place where you got it.'

'I reckon so.'

'Is Raymond's car still there?'

'No, we shall have to get a taxi.'

'Okay,' said Biggles as he settled himself in his seat. 'Better keep low: we don't want to run into a bunch of Zeros.'

The flight to Calcutta was uneventful. On several occasions enemy aircraft were seen, mostly flying high, but the Moth, skimming the tree-tops, escaped observation. By the time it had been moored, and a taxi found, and the trip made to Dum Dum, the sun was low in the western sky. Without stopping to wash or remove the mud from his clothes Biggles walked straight to the mess. The others were waiting.

His first question was, 'How's Angus?'

Algy answered. 'I've been to the hospital—just got back. They wouldn't let me see him—not that there would have been any point in it. He's still unconscious, and likely to remain so. He's badly smashed up—broken arm, broken leg, three ribs stove in and concussion. If he gets over it, it will be months before he's on his feet again. We can reckon him off the strength as far as this show's concerned.'

Biggles shook his head sadly. 'Poor old Angus. Tough luck. Still, it's something that he is still alive. I suppose it was expecting too much to hope that he might have come round. I wanted to talk to him. He might have been able to tell us something—what happened, and how he felt. As far as we know, he's the first victim of the new weapon who has survived, or who has got back.'

'Then you don't know what hit him?' said Bertie.

'I haven't the remotest idea,' admitted Biggles. 'The machine just dived into the drink as if the controls had jammed, or as if he had done it deliberately. That's how it struck me. What do you think, Tug? You saw it.'

'Same as you.'

The others were crowding round. 'You didn't see anything break?' queried Ginger.

'Not a thing,' answered Biggles. 'When the machine hit the water, as far as one could see, there was absolutely nothing wrong with it.'

'What about Moorven's crash?' asked Algy. 'Did you find anything there?'

'Nothing. I'll tell you all about it later, after I've had a bite and a clean up. I really only looked in to get the latest news about Angus. I shall be busy for a bit, making out a written report on Moorven's crash, handing over his effects, and so on. I also want to have a word with Johnny Crisp and Scrimshaw. There's something unnatural about the way they always get back. It can't be luck. There must be a reason, and if we can put our finger on it we shall be half-way towards getting this thing buttoned up.'

At this point Air Commodore Raymond came in. 'I heard you were back.' he announced. 'What happened?'

'Just a minute, sir,' protested Biggles. 'I haven't had anything to eat to-day yet, and blundering about in the jungle was a dirty business—as you can see. Give me a few minutes for a bath and a bite and I'll tell you all about it. Wait here—the others will want to hear the story too. I'll be back.'

In rather less than half an hour he returned, his material needs satisfied. 'Let's sit down,' he suggested.

He then told his story. Narrated in his usual concise manner, it did not take long.

'Then we still haven't got anywhere,' said the Air Commodore despondently.

'I wouldn't say that exactly,' argued Biggles, 'Certain broad aspects are beginning to emerge. When I've had time to think about them I may be able to get a line on the thing.'

'What are you going to do next?'

'It's dark, so there's nothing more we can do in the air. I'd like a word with Crisp and Scrimshaw. There's a bit of a mystery about the way they keep getting back. Of course, it may be luck, but if it isn't, then they, or their machines, must be immune from the thing that's causing the mischief. I'd also like to have a chat with the last man who touched Moorven's machine before he got into it.'

'I've already made inquiries about that,' said the Air Commodore. 'It was a sergeant named Gray. He went over all the machines just before they took off. He seems to be terribly cut up about the three machines going west—somehow feels that they were his responsibility.'

'But that's silly.'

'That's what I told him.'

'What sort of chap is the sergeant?'

'He's a fellow of about thirty, with ten years' service. Exemplary record, and a first class all round fitter-rigger. Before the show, knowing what might happen, he went over every machine, and every engine.'

'I see. Well, we'll leave him till later. Let's get hold of Crisp and Scrimshaw.'

'Where shall we see them—in my office?'

Biggles thought for a moment. 'No. Let's make it informal. I can imagine how they feel. They'll be more likely to open up here than in your office. And I'd like to ask the questions, if you don't mind.'

'Very well,' assented the Air Commodore. 'Get one of your chaps to fetch them. He'll probably find them in the bar at the central mess.'

Biggles raised his eyebrows. 'Drinking?'

'Scrimshaw, who normally doesn't touch anything, is beginning to spend too much time in the bar. It's understandable. After all, these two have watched a squadron wiped out, and some of them have been together since the Battle of Britain.'

Biggles nodded to Ginger. 'Slip along and fetch them,' he ordered.

Ginger went. The others continued the debate for the next few minutes, when Ginger returned with the two officers.

'Sit down, chaps,' invited Biggles quietly. 'Pull up a couple of chairs.'

Crisp and Scrimshaw sat down. Biggles took a quick glance at them in turn as he offered cigarettes. They were both in the condition he expected, for he knew only too well the symptoms resulting from nerve strain, shock, and impotent anger. Scrimshaw's face was flushed and his eyes unnaturally bright. He smoked his cigarette in quick short puffs, tapping it incessantly whether there was any ash on it or not. Crisp was pale but steady; his eyes were a little bloodshot in the corners. The fingers of the hand that took the cigarette shook; the forefinger was yellow with nicotine stain.

'We're trying to get to the bottom of this business,' began Biggles casually.

'Getting time somebody did something about it,' rapped out Scrimshaw.

'No one is likely to argue about that,' replied Biggles gently. 'All is being done that can be done. The Japs have slipped a fast one on us, and the only way we shall get it buttoned up is by keeping our heads. To let it get us on the floor would be playing into their hands.'

'I hear you went down and looked at Moorven?' snapped Scrimshaw.

Biggles looked up. 'Who told you that?'

'I don't know—I heard it.'

'Where did you hear it?'

'In the mess, I expect.'

Biggles glanced round. 'Have you fellows been talking?'

'I don't think anybody has spoken outside this mess,' said Algy. 'In fact, apart from my visit to the hospital I don't think anyone has been out.'

'I remember. It was Lal Din told me,' said Scrimshaw.

Biggles looked at Algy. 'Has Lal Din been here?'

'Yes.'

'When?'

'He served coffee after lunch.'

'I told you not to discuss this thing in front of the staff,' rasped Biggles.

There was an uncomfortable silence.

It was broken by Scrimshaw. 'Pah! What does it matter?'

Biggles ignored the question. 'Let's get on,' he resumed, looking at Crisp and Scrimshaw. 'So far you two fellows have been lucky—'

He winced as Scrimshaw laughed—a harsh, jarring sound.

'Is that your idea of luck?' sneered Scrimshaw.

'All right, Let's say it wasn't luck,' said Biggles

imperturbably. 'Let us say there may be a reason. If we are right in that assumption we soon ought to get the thing pranged.'

'Then you didn't find anything at Moorven's crash?' asked Crisp.

'I found a couple of Japanese soldiers,' returned Biggles.

'What did you do with them?' demanded Scrimshaw.

'I shot them,' answered Biggles evenly.

Scrimshaw let out a yell. 'By thunder! I wish I'd been there. I'd have—'

'Maybe you'll get a chance to do even better later on,' interrupted Biggles curtly. 'I baled out over Moorven's crash to-day hoping to find out whether the new weapon strikes at the man or the machine. Unfortunately there was no indication. What I'm trying to find out now is, what you two fellows did that Moorven did not do. Conversely, what he did that you did not do. It may have been something that happened in the air or on the ground. I should have liked to put this same question to one of my flight commanders, who bought it this morning, but unfortunately he is not yet able to speak. Johnny, I want you to think very carefully and tell me everything you did from the moment you got up this morning.'

'Where's that going to get us?' demanded Scrimshaw, lighting a fresh cigarette from the one he already held.

'It may get us nowhere,' admitted Biggles. 'But let's look at it this way. Only one thing is quite certain. Either our machines are being attacked by something we can't see, or the pilots in them. I'm going to deal with both possibilities in turn. Right now I am working on the personal aspect. Go ahead Johnny.'

'I got out of bed,' began Crisp. 'I took off my pyjamas

and dressed.'

'Didn't you wash or have a bath?'

'No.'

'Go on.'

'I then went over to the mess, where I stood by the big table and had some coffee and biscuits.'

'Was anyone else there?'

'Not when I got there. The others came in later.'

'And what did they do?'

'They joined me at the table.'

'And had coffee and biscuits?'

'Yes.'

'You're sure of that?'

'Scrimshaw's here, ask him.'

'That's right,' said Scrimshaw shortly. 'We all had coffee and biscuits. Nothing funny about that, was there?'

'Nothing at all,' agreed Biggles calmly. 'And this coffee all came out of the same pot?'

'Yes,' Crisp answered.

'What about the biscuits?'

'We all helped ourselves from the same plate.'

'And there was nobody else in the room all this time—I mean staff?'

'Nobody. The stuff is put out and anybody who wants can help himself. That's the usual arrangement.'

'Go on,' invited Biggles.

'The five of us then walked over to the machines together.'

'Did you smoke after finishing the coffee?'

'Sorry—yes. I forgot that. I had a packet of cigarettes in my pocket. Being finished first I had one, and passed the packet.'

'Then you all smoked cigarettes from the same packet?'

'What's all this?' snapped Scrimshaw. 'Are you trying to make out—'

'Take it easy,' interrupted Biggles. 'I'm not trying to make out anything. I'm asking for facts. Go ahead, Johnny.'

'That's all. We got into our machines and took off.'

'You didn't touch anything else?'

'No.'

'Did you speak to anyone?'

'Yes, I spoke to the sergeant—Sergeant Gray.'

'What about?'

Johnny looked uncomfortable. 'About the change-over.'

'What change-over?'

'Well, you see, I swopped planes with Moorven.'

'You *what*?'

'Changed planes.'

'Why?'

'Well, I reckoned perhaps somebody was tinkering with the machines, but for some reason or other mine was always left alone. We decided to change kites to see what happened. If I went west*, and Moorven got back, it would begin to look as if there was some peculiarity about my machine that was saving me all the time. It was because of this that I feel so rotten now. If poor old Moorven had stuck to his own machine he would have got back.'

'You mean—he *might* have got back,' said Biggles softly. 'I understand, Johnny. What you really did was to take a big chance of going west yourself. That was pretty noble of you. I'm glad you mentioned this because it rather goes to prove that the machine doesn't make any difference, and that's important. Sergeant

* Slang: got killed.

79

Gray knew about this change?'

'Yes.'

Biggles turned to Scrimshaw. 'Did you speak to anybody?'

'Not a soul.'

'And in the air neither of you did anything beyond controlling the aircraft?'

Scrimshaw laughed mirthlessly. 'What else was there to do?'

'I don't know,' answered Biggles. 'That's what I'm trying to find out. You say you both did nothing, so that settles that. And neither of you at any time heard or felt the slightest thing, no noise, no jar, nothing unusual?'

'Nothing at all,' said Johnny.

'That goes for me too,' added Scrimshaw.

'Not even when Moorven fell out of position?' queried Biggles.

'No.'

'You saw him go, of course?'

'Yes, we both saw him go,' confirmed Johnny.

'Moorven didn't say anything over the radio?'

'Not a word.'

'Did you speak to him?'

'Yes. I called him, and asked him what he was doing.'

'Didn't he answer?'

'No.'

'And the others went down in similar circumstances?'

'Yes. Grainger fell about ten minutes after Moorven went, but Larkin lasted nearly all the way home. He went down about five miles inside the Jap lines.'

'I see—thanks.' Biggles looked at the Air Commodore. 'Any questions you would like to ask?'

The Air Commodore shook his head. 'No. I think

you've covered the ground pretty thoroughly. There's just one thing, though.' He looked at Crisp and Scrimshaw. 'What are you two fellows going to do? Your squadron is washed out for the time being. Would you like a spot of leave?'

'Not for me, sir,' answered Scrimshaw. 'Leave is the last thing I want.'

'And me,' added Johnny. 'We'll go on flying till we hit the deck or get to the bottom of this thing, one or the other.'

'It won't do either of you any good to go on living in an empty mess,' suggested the Air Commodore gently. 'Bigglesworth has to-day lost one of his flight commanders. Crisp, why don't you let me attach you, temporarily, to his squadron, to fill the gap? I'm sure he'd be glad to have you. And you, too, Scrimshaw. You'll work better if you have someone to talk things over with.'

'Yes, why not?' put in Biggles quickly.

The two pilots looked at each other.

'That suits me fine,' said Johnny. 'That is, if Scrim. will come over?'

'I'll come anywhere.' muttered Scrimshaw. 'It's all the same to me.'

'It may be, but it isn't all the same to me,' said Biggles coldly. 'The boys in this squadron have covered a lot of sky since the war started, and it wouldn't be fair to them to turn in more risks then they normally take. Frankly, Scrimshaw, we haven't much confidence in fellows who grab a bottle when things get sticky.'

Scrimshaw flushed scarlet. 'Who said—'

'I said,' broke in Biggles without raising his voice. 'And what I say I mean. The sooner you understand that the better. Oh, I know how you feel. I've been through it myself, more than once. I was going through it when you wore safety-pins instead of buttons, but I got over it—if I hadn't I shouldn't be here now. If you go on ginning-up you'll be no use to yourself or anyone else. We needn't say any more about it—but think it over. Make a party with my fellows after dinner and take a trip round the town. They'll do anything you want to do, but they don't brood and they don't booze—those are the only two things we bar. We've too much to do. That's all for now.' Biggles got up.

8

Death Marches on

As the officers dispersed, talking over the mystery quietly among themselves, Biggles turned to Air Commodore Raymond. 'I think I shall go along right away and have a word or two with Sergeant Gray, sir,' he announced. 'There's just time before dinner.'

'Do you mind if I come with you?' asked Johnny Crisp. 'It's partly my pigeon. Gray is in A Flight—my flight.'

'Come by all means—only too glad to have you along, invited Biggles. 'He'll probably say more to you than to strangers. That'll be enough, though, we don't want a crowd.'

Biggles, the Air Commodore and Johnny, left the officers' quarters and walked along to the sergeants' mess, where they learned that Sergeant Gray was out.

'Any idea where he is?' Biggles asked the flight sergeant who had come to the door.

'I think I heard him say something about going down to the flight shed, sir,' returned the flight sergeant. 'He wanted to have another look at those two machines that got back this morning.'

'Thanks,' acknowledged Biggles. 'Maybe we'll find him there.'

'I hope he isn't going to let this thing prey on his mind,' remarked Johnny, as they walked on to the hangar in which the two surviving A Flight machines were parked. 'He's a good chap. He's been in the squadron pretty nearly since it was formed at Kenley years ago.'

The hangar was in darkness. The Air Commodore switched on a torch. The beam fell on the two Hurricanes, but there was no one with them.

'Anyone about?' called Biggles.

There was no answer.

Biggles saw a narrow crack of light half-way down and on one side of the building. 'That must be him, in the flight office,' he observed.

They walked on to the door. Biggles opened it. He stopped. 'Take a look at this,' he murmured dryly.

Lying on the floor, breathing stertorously, was a sergeant.

'That's Gray,' said Johnny. 'Drunk as a lord, by the look of it.'

'You seem pretty sure of that,' challenged Biggles.

'He's done it before. The same thing happened last week. If I'd put him on a charge he'd have lost his stripes, and I hate doing that to a good airman. I made him promise he wouldn't do it again.'

'Does he make a habit of doing this sort of thing?' asked the Air Commodore.

'Not as far as I know,' replied Johnny. 'I think he's only taken to it lately. Pity.'

Biggles shook the sergeant by the shoulder. 'Come on, snap out of it,' he ordered peremptorily.

The sergeant did not move.

'Get up, Gray,' snapped Johnny irritably.

The sergeant lay still, snoring.

Biggles pommelled him, and in the end slapped his face.

The sergeant grunted, but did not move.

'He certainly has got a skinful,' muttered Johnny. 'He sort of went to pieces when I told him that Moorven and the others had gone west, but I didn't think he'd take it like this.' He shook the sergeant again.

'It's no use,' said Biggles quietly. 'We shan't get anything out of him in that state. There's only one thing that might bring him round. Slip over to the mess, Johnny, and get a jug of black coffee, hot.'

Johnny went off at a run.

While they were waiting, the Air Commodore spoke to Biggles. 'What do you really make of all this?'

'It's fantastic—that's the only word for it,' replied Biggles. 'What beats me is, the thing is so infernally inconsistent. To-day, Tug made three trips well into enemy country and got away with it every time. Why? How? There must be an answer to that, if only we could hit on it. There were a lot of enemy machines about; I saw them, yet they weren't affected. They flew as if they had nothing to fear. Very strange. I have a feeling, not based on anything concrete, that—'

Johnny came in, slightly breathless from his run. 'There was no black coffee on tap, so I ordered some,' he announced. 'Lal Din says he will bring it over right away.' He looked at the sergeant. 'Silly fool, letting the flight down like this.'

A minute or two later the steward came in. His habitual smile broadened when his eyes fell on the sergeant.

'He catch plenty whisky,' he chuckled. 'Here coffee, sahib. Velly stlong.'

Biggles took the coffee-pot, a small copper one, from the tray, and walked over to the sergeant. 'What part of the world do you come from, Lal Din?' he asked casually. 'You don't talk like a man of this country.'

'Me Burmese. I blong Mandalay,' was the answer.

'You don't look much like a Burman,' said Biggles without looking up, as he dropped on his knees beside the unconscious N.C.O*.

* Non-Commissioned Officer eg a Sergeant or Corporal.

'Father Burman, but he dead long time. Mother, she Chinese. Bling me up China fashion,' said Lal Din.

Biggles forced the N.C.O.'s teeth apart, not without difficulty, and poured coffee into the mouth.

The sergeant spluttered. Biggles looked over his shoulder at Lal Din, who was still standing just inside the door. 'What are you waiting for?' he asked sharply.

'I wait for coffee-pot, sahib. Canteen ploperty. Maybe someone else want coffee.'

'You can fetch it later on. We may be some time.'

'Velly good, sahib.' Lal Din went off.

'What's the matter with him? Don't you trust him?' asked the Air Commodore.

'In a show like this, the only people I trust are those I know,' answered Biggles, pouring more coffee into the sergeant's mouth.

Again the sergeant spluttered, chokingly. His head lolled from side to side. His eyes opened.

'Come on Gray; pull yourself together,' rapped out Biggles tersely.

'Wash-washer matter?' gasped the sergeant.

'You're drunk,' said Johnny bitingly.

The sergeant was indignant. 'Thash a lie. Not drunk.'

Biggles gave him more coffee.

'He says he isn't drunk,' said Johnny, looking at Biggles and the Air Commodore in turn.

'Of course he does.' The Air Commodore laughed lugubriously. 'Did you ever know a drunken man admit that he was tight? I didn't.'

'If you tell him he's drunk he'll spend the rest of the night trying to prove that he isn't,' put in Biggles wearily.

The sergeant's eyes were clearing. 'Wash wrong?' he demanded in a dazed voice, and was then violently sick.

'Tight as an owl,' muttered Johnny. 'You won't get any sense out of him till he's slept it off.'

'I'm afraid you're right,' agreed Biggles sadly. 'What a nuisance.' He shook the sergeant again. 'Listen to me, Gray. Can you hear what I say?'

'Yes—shir.'

'That's better. We'll talk to you later.'

'Don't wanner talk—hic. Those swine killed my officers. I wanner get at 'em. You hear me? I wanner—'

Biggles stood up. 'Yes, we know. You go to your bunk and sleep it off.'

'Schleep what off?' slurred the sergeant drowsily.

'You're all ginned-up,' put in Johnny, who was getting more and more angry. 'You promised me you wouldn't touch the stuff.'

'Drunk! Hark at him,' pleaded the sergeant. 'Says I'm drunk. I was never drunk—in my life—no shir.'

'We'll settle that argument later,' averred Biggles, arranging a packed parachute under the sergeant's head. 'Have a sleep. Here, you might as well finish the rest of the coffee.'

Without assistance the N.C.O. took the remainder of the coffee at a gulp. 'Thash berrer,' he declared sleepily. 'I just wanner be alone,' he rambled on. 'I only came here to be alone. Sat here, chewing the thing over, thas all. I may be sick, but I ain't drunk—no shir.'

'Silly ass,' muttered Johnny.

'I wouldn't be too hard on him,' said Biggles as they went out. 'His nerves are probably in rags. You say he's been with the squadron a long time? Well, now he's seen the squadron washed out. He ought to be sent home for a rest.'

'I'll get him posted,' promised the Air Commodore.

They went to the mess and had dinner. Later, after listening to the news on the radio, they sat in a corner with Algy and Bertie discussing the mystery from all angles, without, however, coming any nearer to solving it. Biggles said little. Eventually he looked at his watch.

'Eleven o'clock,' he announced. 'I think I shall turn in, and leave Sergeant Gray until to-morrow.'

'I'll just walk down and make sure he's all right,' offered Johnny.

'Be as well,' agreed Biggles.

The Air Commodore got up. 'I'll be getting along, too,' he decided. 'See you in the morning.' He nodded to the others and departed.

Johnny went off. Biggles stood for a minute or two talking to Algy and Ginger, who wanted to know if he had made any plans for the following day. He told them he wanted to do some more thinking before he decided on a definite programme.

He was walking along the path that led to the officers' sleeping quarters when an airman overtook him.

'Excuse me, sir, you're wanted on the 'phone,' said he.

'Which 'phone?' asked Biggles.

'The one in the hall, sir.'

Biggles turned back. 'Where have you just come from?' he asked.

'I was on duty in the kitchen, sir.'

'I see.' Biggles stepped into the hall and picked up the telephone.

'Is that you, Biggles?' said a voice. 'This is Johnny here. I'd like you to come down to the flight shed.'

'Something wrong?' queried Biggles.

'Yes, it's the sergeant.'

'Is he still there?'

'Yes.'

'Is something wrong with him?'

'Plenty,' said Johnny. 'He's dead.'

'Stay there,' said Biggles tersely. 'I'll be right down.'

Biggles ran to the shed. Johnny was there, alone, bending over the sergeant, who was lying on his back on the floor, the position in which they had left him. One glance at the open mouth and staring eyes was enough.

'He's a goner all right,' said Biggles in a hard voice. He shook his head. 'I don't get it. He was coming round fast when we left him. Well, there goes my hope of learning anything from him. I wonder why he died? You've had a look at him I suppose?'

'Of course. Can't find a thing. Not a wound, not a mark of any sort. Can't make it out. He must have passed out in a drunken stupor.'

'Well, there's nothing we can do except send for the doctor,' said Biggles.

'I wonder if he did himself in, in a fit of remorse?' suggested Johnny.

'I imagine it is very difficult to commit suicide without leaving some sign of it,' returned Biggles. 'Go and fetch the M.O.*'

Johnny departed on his errand.

After gazing at the body for a moment or two Biggles looked round the little room, his eyes taking in everything. Nothing had been disturbed. The room appeared to be precisely as when he had last seen it. The coffee-pot and the tray were still there. He went to the pot and picked it up. It was empty. Thoughtfully, he put it down again. For a while he did not move from where he stood; then his eyes stopped on a tiny object that lay on the floor near the waste-paper basket. A quick

* Medical Officer.

step took him to it. Stooping, he picked it up. It was a round pellet of paper, pink. Slowly he unfolded it and found in his hand a slip of grease-proof paper, about three inches square. There was printing on one side. He read it: WITH THE COMPLIMENTS OF CHARNEYS LTD., LONDON. NOT FOR SALE. SUPPLIED FOR THE USE OF H.M. FORCES ONLY. With a frown lining his forehead he raised the paper to his nostrils. His eyes switched to the dead N.C.O. He went over to him, and dropping on his knees, looked into his eyes.

There came a sound of quick footsteps and the M.O. entered, followed by Johnny. Ignoring Biggles the doctor went straight to the body. Silence settled in the death chamber while he examined it. After a while he stood up. 'I'll get him over to the mortuary,' he said.

'What do you make of it?' asked Biggles.

'I'd rather reserve my opinion till after the post-mortem examination,' replied the doctor.

'There'll be an autopsy?'

'Of course.' The doctor looked at Johnny. 'He was in your flight, wasn't he?'

'Yes.'

'Can you offer an explanation of this?'

'We found him here, drunk, about three hours ago,' answered Johnny. 'We left him in the same state. He was badly cut up about the casualties to-day.'

'Have you known him to get drunk before?'

'Yes. I had him on the mat for the same thing about a week ago. But surely, Doc, booze doesn't *kill* a man?'

'In the East, in the sort of weather we've been having lately, it can induce heat stroke, which does. More often, though, the man runs amok. In that condition he often tries to commit suicide. You'd better go, now. I'm going to lock the door till the ambulance comes to collect the body.'

They went out. The M.O. locked the door.

'Where are you going now, Johnny?' asked Biggles.

'I think I shall push along to bed.'

'Me too,' said Biggles.

'Mind if I tell Scrimshaw about this?'

'Not in the least,' answered Biggles. 'I'll see you in the morning. Good night. Good night, Doc.'

Biggles walked on alone. He did not go straight to his quarter, but walked slowly to the sergeants' mess, where he sent for the mess secretary and the barman. He took them outside.

'Sergeant Gray has just been found dead,' he announced quietly. 'He looked as though he had been drinking. Did he have anything here before he went out?'

'I didn't see him at the bar,' said the mess secretary—a warrant officer.

'Yes, he came, but he didn't stay,' volunteered the barman. 'I served him with an iced lemonade—I think it was. I know it was a soft drink because someone pulled his leg about it. Then he said he was going down to the sheds. I recall that because the flight sergeant told him it didn't do any good to mope about.'

'Did Gray seem at all agitated or upset?'

'No, sir, I can't say that he did. I didn't take much notice of him, but from what I remember he was quieter than usual.'

'Thanks,' said Biggles. 'That's all I wanted to know.'

Deep in thought he turned away and went to his quarter. For a long time he sat on his bed, thinking, smoking cigarettes. Then he undressed and got between the sheets.

Chapter 9
Biggles Plays Fox

The following morning Biggles was up early. Before doing anything else he called the hospital on the telephone to inquire about Angus. He learned that his condition was the same; he was still unconscious.

Before he had finished dressing there was a tap on the door and Air Commodore Raymond came in. He looked worn with worry. 'I've just heard about Sergeant Gray,' he said in a tired voice. 'This is awful. What do you suggest we do?'

'For a start, sir, I'd advise you to ask the doctor to give you something to help you to sleep, or you'll be the next casualty.'

'How can I sleep with this horror hanging over my head?' said the Air Commodore. 'What do you make of this business of Gray?'

'I have an uncomfortable feeling that we're partly responsible for that,' returned Biggles, without looking round. He was washing out his shaving kit.

'What on earth do you mean?'

'We were too ready to take it for granted that he was drunk.'

'Wasn't he?'

'No. At least, I don't think so, unless he got the stuff outside somewhere. The indications are that he didn't leave the station.'

'How do you know that?'

'I made it my business to find out.'

'If he wasn't drunk, then what was the matter with

him?'

'Why waste time guessing? The M.O. is holding an autopsy. Presumably it will be this morning, since it is customary here to bury people on the same day as they die. We shall soon know the truth—I hope.'

'There's a rumour about the station that it was suicide.'

Biggles flicked his tie angrily. 'How did *that* start? Rumour—rumour—rumour ... always rumours. If people only knew the harm they do. I'd like to know who started this one.'

'You're not suggesting that it was started deliberately?'

'That wouldn't surprise me. Rumour is a weapon in this war.'

'You don't believe this one, evidently?'

'I prefer to keep an open mind until after the autopsy.'

'If he didn't die from natural causes then it must have been suicide.'

Biggles put on his tunic. 'It doesn't seem to have occurred to you that it might have been murder.'

'Murder!' The Air Commodore looked aghast.

'That's what I said.'

'But what possible motive could anyone have for murdering a harmless fellow like Gray?'

Biggles lit a cigarette. 'The same motive that cost Moorven and the others their lives.'

'I don't understand.'

'The man who was responsible for Moorven's death wanted Japan to win the war. It may be that the man who killed Gray—if Gray was, in fact, murdered—was actuated by the same desire.'

'But why Gray?'

'You seem to forget that Gray was A Flight fitter;

93

that he was the last man to look over the three machines that were lost yesterday, and that we were waiting to interrogate him. If Gray could have talked he might have told us something, something that might have put us on the track of the secret weapon. If that were so, then there was ample motive for killing him.'

'I didn't think of that,' murmured Raymond.

'Don't breathe a word of it to anyone,' adjured Biggles. 'I mean that seriously and literally. It's only my opinion. Let's wait for the result of the autopsy before we start barking up what may turn out to be the wrong tree.'

'I shan't say anything,' said the Air Commodore heavily. 'I've another worry now.'

'What is it this time?'

'The rot has started at another station.'

Biggles turned sharply. 'Where?'

'Darwin, Australia. They lost five machines yester-day out of one formation—all down in the sea. It's clear that unless we can stop it, the thing will spread over the entire Pacific. We've got to work fast. Biggles-worth.'

'You flatter me,' returned Biggles curtly. 'The whole Intelligence Branch has been working on this thing for weeks yet you expect me to produce results in twenty-four hours. Have a heart.' He finished dressing and picked up his cap.

'Where are you going now?' asked the Air Commo-dore despondently.

'To get some breakfast. It's a good thing to eat, sometimes.'

'And then?'

'I'm going to take out a patrol.'

'Good God, man! You can't do that!' objected the

94

Air Commodore in a startled voice.

'Why not?'

'Because you're our one hope now. If anything happens to you—'

'It'll be worse for me than it will for you,' interposed Biggles dryly. 'The thing won't come to *us*. We've got to find it.'

'Are you taking the whole squadron out?'

'No.' Biggles smiled faintly. 'I'll leave some for tomorrow—in case.'

Algy came in. He saluted the Air Commodore and looked at Biggles. 'What's the programme?'

'I'll tell you over breakfast. I'll be across in a minute. Do something for me.'

'What is it?'

'I'm smoking too much. Walk along to the canteen and buy me a packet of chewing-gum.'

'Okay.'

'What am I going to tell Darwin?' asked the Air Commodore.

'I may be able to suggest something later in the day,' answered Biggles, putting his map in his pocket. 'Meantime, I'll push along.'

At the door they parted, the Air Commodore returning to headquarters and Biggles walking over to the dining-room, where he found the rest of the squadron, including the new members, Johnny and Scrimshaw, already gathered, drinking coffee and munching biscuits from a large plate. Before joining them he rang the bell.

Lal Din, smiling, obsequious, answered it.

'Listen, chaps, this is the programme for this morning,' announced Biggles. Then, noticing the steward, he said, 'Bring me a packet of cigarettes.'

'Yes, sahib.' Lal Din went out.

Biggles poured a cup of coffee, spread his map on the table and looked at it for a minute or two. 'We're going to do a sortie,' he went on. 'I shan't be going myself. I'm not sending the whole squadron—just two machines. Johnny and Ginger can go. One reason for that is I don't want a mixed formation. We'll use two Hurricanes. You, Johnny, will fly X M, which leaves X T for Ginger. The others, for the moment, will have to stay on the ground. This will be the course. After taking off the two machines will head east for an hour. That will take them into the area where the machines were lost yesterday, and not far from where Angus went down. They will then turn north for fifteen minutes, after which they will return home.' Biggles looked at Johnny and Ginger. 'Is that clear?'

They nodded.

'All right, then.' Biggles looked at his watch. 'You will leave the ground in twenty minutes. Finish your coffee. There's no immediate hurry.' He looked round. 'Where's that man with my cigarettes? Ah! There you are, Lal Din. Thanks.' Biggles took the cigarettes from the proffered tray and signed the chit.

The steward went out.

Biggles lit a cigarette and sipped his coffee. Then he beckoned to Algy and took him on one side. 'Did you get that chewing-gum?'

'Yes.' Algy produced the tiny package and handed it over.

Biggles glanced at it and dropped it in his pocket. 'I've got a job for you,' he said in a low voice. 'Don't say a word about it to anyone, either here or anywhere else. I want you to go first of all to the M.O. and ask him to give you something guaranteed to make a man sick. If he jibs, go to Raymond. But if you tell him it's for me I think he'll let you have it—he knows I'm on a special job. You will then borrow the reserve ambulance, and driving it yourself, take it to the practice landing-ground at Gayhar. That's a little place among the paddy-fields about six miles north of here. You'd better push off right away, because I want you to be at Gayhar inside an hour.'

Algy's eyes had opened wide while Biggles was giving these instructions, but he did not question them. 'Have you got a line on something?' he breathed.

'I think so,' answered Biggles softly. 'This is really an experiment to test a theory.'

'What am I to do at Gayhar?'

'Nothing. Just sit on the edge of the field and wait.'

'Wait for what?'

'For me. Push off now.'

Algy went out, and Biggles returned to the others who—probably to conceal their real feelings—were making joking remarks about the two pilots detailed for the patrol. He sat down and finished his coffee. Some minutes later he again looked at his watch.

'All right, you chaps, you'd better get along now. I'll walk down with you and see you off. The rest will stay here till I come back. I may need you.'

With Johnny and Ginger he walked towards the machines, which were being wheeled out on to the tarmac. 'What a grand day,' he remarked. 'I think I'll come with you, after all. I'll fly a Spit.'

'You will!' cried Ginger delightedly.

'Yes.'

'I'm glad you've changed your mind,' remarked Johnny.

'As a matter of fact I haven't,' returned Biggles evenly. 'I intended coming all along.'

Johnny stared. 'Then why didn't you say so?'

'Because I am getting nervous of letting too many

people know my movements,' declared Biggles. 'I want you two fellows to remember what you're doing and keep your wits about you. The moment either of you feels anything happening to you, let me know—if you can.'

'You mean, when we get into enemy country?' queried Johnny.

'No. We're not going into enemy country. We're going to stop this side of the lines.'

Johnny pulled up dead. 'Then what's the idea of this sortie?'

'The idea is,' replied Biggles, 'if either of you falls out I'd rather it were where I can get at you.'

Johnny looked astonished. 'But what *can* happen, this side of the lines?'

'You may be surprised,' answered Biggles vaguely.

'But what about you?' put in Ginger. 'You talk as though something might happen to us, but not to you.'

'If my guess is right, I don't think it can,' answered Biggles. 'That's enough questions. We're not going far—only to Gayhar landing field. When we get there we shall land, and just sit in our seats for a couple of hours, leaving the engines running. Conditions will then be the same as if we were up topsides, only our wheels will be on the carpet. I'm afraid it's going to be rather boring, but it may be worth it. Let's go.'

The three machines, two Hurricanes and a Spitfire, took off in formation, with Biggles heading due east for a time, as if they were bound for Burma. But as soon as he had satisfied himself that they were out of sight of the airfield he swung round, and in a few minutes had the flight circling over the practice landing-ground.

Ginger spoke over the radio. 'What's that blood-wagon* doing down there?'

Biggles answered: 'I suppose somebody thinks it may be needed. That's enough talking.'

He continued circling for a little while and then went down. The three machines landed as they had taken off, and finished within a short distance of each other. And in that position they remained, the motors throttled back, the airscrews ticking over.

After an hour had passed Biggles got out and walked over to Ginger's machine. Having climbed up on the wing he asked, 'Are you still feeling all right?'

'Right as rain,' answered Ginger.

'Stay where you are,' ordered Biggles, and went over to Johnny.

'Are you still feeling all right?' he inquired.

'I'm getting a bit browned off, otherwise okay.'

'Stay where you are.'

Biggles returned to his Spitfire and resumed his seat in the cockpit.

Another hour—a long, weary hour—passed. Again Biggles got out and went over to Ginger. 'Still feeling all right?'

'Never felt better,' declared Ginger. 'This is a slow game, Biggles. How long is it going on?'

'Stay where you are,' commanded Biggles, and went on to the other Hurricane, increasing his pace when he noted that Johnny's head was sagging on his chest as if he were asleep. He jumped on a wing. 'Johnny!' he shouted.

Johnny did not answer.

Biggles touched him. Johnny lolled, limply.

Biggles moved fast. He switched off the engine and

* Slang: ambulance

99

dashed back to Ginger. 'All right!' he shouted. 'Switch off. Johnny's bought it. Come over and help me to get him down.' Then, turning towards the ambulance he raised his arms above his head, beckoning. As soon as the vehicle started forward he ran back to Johnny's Hurricane, and, with Ginger's help, got the unconscious pilot to the ground. By the time this had been accomplished Algy had brought the ambulance to the stop, and had joined the little party.

'Bear a hand, Algy. Let's get him into the blood-cart,' said Biggles tersely. He had turned a trifle pale.

They lifted Johnny on to one of the stretchers.

'Did you get that stuff from the doctor?' Biggles asked Algy.

'Yes. He says it would make an elephant heave its heart out.'

'Let's have it—quick.'

Algy handed him a bottle.

Biggles tore the cork out with his teeth and coaxed a little of the liquid the bottle contained between Johnny's pallid lips.

Johnny spluttered. He gasped. He retched. Then he was sick.

'Okay,' said Biggles softly. 'Keep that blanket over him to keep him warm.'

Johnny was sick again. Panting, he opened his eyes. They were dull, with the pupils dilated. He was sick again.

'Pass the water, Algy,' ordered Biggles. He wiped Johnny's face and bathed the temples. 'There should be some smelling-salts in that first-aid cabinet,' he told Ginger.

Ginger brought the bottle.

Johnny gasped as the pungent fumes struck his nostrils, but they hastened his recovery.

'What—what was it?' he gasped.

'Take your time, old lad—you'll soon be okay,' said Biggles soothingly.

Johnny's eyes cleared, and he was soon able to sit up.

'Feel well enough to tell us what happened?' asked Biggles.

'Yes, I think so. My God! It was awful.'

'Lucky your wheels were on the floor, eh?'

'If they hadn't been—I should—have come a crumper.* Is this—what got—the others?'

Biggles nodded. 'Tell us what happened.'

Johnny had another drink of water. 'Well, I just sat there for what seemed a long time,' he explained. 'Then I felt a queer sort of feeling coming over me. At first I thought it was the heat; then I realised it wasn't. But by that time I was too far gone to do anything about it. It was hell. Phew! Does my head rock! It feels as if there were a couple of pistons inside it.'

'That'll pass off,' said Biggles. 'Go on with the story.'

'I thought I was dying,' continued Johnny. 'Everything round me was all distorted. I had a feeling I was flying upside-down. The instruments were all heaped in a pile. I tried to move, to call you on the radio, but I couldn't. My bones had all gone to jelly. Then I couldn't make out what things were—they sort of flowed about into each other, as if they were liquid. They turned all colours.'

'But you were still conscious?'

'I can't say I knew what was happening. The pain in my head was terrible. It felt as if my brain had split into two parts. One part was mad, and the other part a sort of spectator. I couldn't do anything—couldn't

* Slang: crashed

make a sound. That's the last I remember. I suppose I must have passed out. The thought of that happening in the air makes my skin curl. What was it? Do you know?'

'I think so,' answered Biggles. 'I fancy it was the piece of chewing-gum you ate.'

Johnny stared at Biggles' face. 'Chewing-gum?' he ejaculated. 'What chewing-gum?'

Biggles' expression changed to one of questioning surprise. 'Didn't you find a packet of chewing-gum in the pocket of your instrument panel, and put a piece in your mouth?'

'No. I hate the stuff, anyway.'

Biggles looked incredulous. 'Are you *sure*?'

A smile, faintly sarcastic, curled Johnny's lips. 'Dash it all! I may look dumb, but I'm not so cheesed that I don't know when I chew gum. I tell you, I never touch the stuff.'

Biggles bit his lip, looking really crestfallen. 'If that's the case I'm on the wrong trail after all. I still don't understand it though. Are you absolutely positive that there was no gum in your cockpit?'

'Not to-day.'

'What do you mean by that, exactly? Does it imply that you have had some gum in your cockpit on other occasions?'

'There usually is a piece. It's a free issue, you know. Might almost call it normal equipment.'

'You find it in the machine when you get in?'

'Yes.'

'Who puts it there?'

'Sergeant Gray used to. He sort of did the round before the show.'

'But there was no gum in your machine to-day? Why not, I wonder?'

'Probably because I told Gray yesterday morning that he was wasting his time putting it in.'

Biggles looked at Ginger. 'Wasn't there any gum in your machine, either?'

'No.'

An expression of baffled bewilderment came over Biggles' face. He shrugged his shoulders helplessly. 'This is a bone-shaker,' he said in a disappointed voice. 'Everything turned out just as I thought it would, except that I expected Ginger to be the one to crack up. I've gone wrong somewhere—or else the devils have been too smart for me. I would have bet my life that I was on the right track. I'd more or less proved it—as I thought—this morning. I offered you a piece of chewing gum—Algy had got it for me from the canteen. You refused. I offered Scrimshaw a piece. He refused, too—told me he never touched the stuff. I was suspicious of chewing-gum, and when I discovered that neither you nor Scrimshaw touched the stuff it seemed to confirm my theory—that the stuff was phoney. I was convinced that you and Scrimshaw always got back because, by a lucky chance for you, neither of you chewed gum. By passing out this morning, Johnny, you've knocked my theory sideways.'

'What set you on this chewing-gum line of argument?' asked Ginger curiously.

Biggles took a small square of pink paper from his pocket and showed it to Johnny. 'This is the stuff the gum is packed in, isn't it? Really, I needn't ask you, because I bought a packet this morning.'

'That's right,' agreed Johnny.

'I found a piece of this paper in Moorven's machine. That told me he had been chewing-gum in the cockpit. I paid no attention to it at the time—after all, there was nothing remarkable about it. But when, last night,

I found a piece of the same paper in A Flight office, where Gray was lying apparently drunk, I began to think. When I learned from the sergeants' mess that Gray had had nothing to drink there, I thought still harder. I thought I was on the track. When, this morning, as I have said, I learned that you and Scrimshaw, the survivors of a squadron, never touched gum, my surmise began to look a certainty. Now it looks as though the gum has nothing to do with it . . . but I still think there's something queer about it.'

'Since Gray is dead, he couldn't very well put gum into any of the machines this morning,' Algy pointed out.

'That's true enough,' admitted Biggles. 'And I'm afraid that settles the argument. There was no gum— yet Johnny passes out. Obviously, it wasn't gum that did the trick.' He sat down on the end of the stretcher and lit a cigarette.

'Well, there was certainly no gum in my machine,' declared Ginger. 'If there had been I should probably have nibbled a piece. I was getting pretty browned off, sitting there doing nothing.'

For a little while Biggles sat with his chin in his hand, deep in thought. Then he got up. 'Stay where you are,' he ordered. 'I'm just going to have a look round these machines.' He went off, climbing first into the cockpit of Johnny's machine, and then treating Ginger's in like manner. He was not long away. 'All right,' he said briskly when he returned. 'We may as well get back to Dum Dum. Don't mention this business to anyone, nor even speak of it among yourselves in the mess. I don't think you're quite fit to fly yet, Johnny, so you'd better trundle back in the blood-wagon. Do you feel well enough to drive it?'

'Yes, I'm all right now,' answered Johnny. In spite

of his assurance he still looked somewhat shaken.

'Fine. Algy will fly your machine home. Let's go.'

Biggles walked over to his aircraft, and after waiting for Algy and Ginger to get into position, took off.

Chapter 10
The Blitz That Failed

When Biggles landed at Dum Dum, and taxied in, he observed with mounting curiosity that the airfield was, to use the common Air Force expression, in a state of flap. Airmen were running about, orders were being shouted, and engines roared as aircraft were dispersed all round the perimeter of the airfield. Having stepped down, he was gazing with mild surprise at this spectacle, when Air Commodore Raymond, followed by Group Captain Boyle, the station commander, came hurrying to him.

'Thank heaven you're back,' began the Air Commodore in a tense voice. 'You're the very man I want to see.'

'What the dickens is going on here?' asked Biggles.

'We're in for a pasting, I'm afraid—and Calcutta, too, no doubt,' asserted the Air Commodore, pulling a wry face. 'We've just had a signal from our forward observers to the effect that the biggest formation of Jap bombers seen in this part of the world is heading in this direction. Ninety-eight of 'em. We suppose they're taking advantage of the situation created by the secret weapon to have a really good smack at us. They know we are powerless to stop them.'

'You mean, they *think* we are,' returned Biggles grimly. 'How far away is this formation?'

'They'll be here in twenty minutes.'

'What are they?'

'Mitsubishi bombers.'

'Any escort?'

'No. They have good reason for thinking they don't need one.'

'What are you doing about it?'

'We're sending up six fighters to intercept them.'

'Six! What do you suppose six machines are going to do against that mob? Why only six? There are more fighters than that on the station.'

'I know, but we daren't leave ourselves without a reserve. With this secret weapon operating I don't suppose we shall see any of our machines again.'

Biggles pointed at a pathetically small formation of Spitfires just taking off. 'Are those the six?'

'Yes.'

'Stop them. Call them back.'

'But—'

'I know what I'm doing, sir. Recall them.'

The Air Commodore hesitated. 'But if Calcutta is bombed—'

'You're going the right way to get it bombed,' broke in Biggles impatiently. 'Look, sir, we've no time to waste in argument or explanations. If you'll leave this operation to me I promise you won't regret it.'

'But think—'

'I've never let you down yet, have I?'

The Air Commodore decided. 'All right.' He turned to the Group Captain. 'Recall those machines.'

The Group Captain hurried off, and in a few seconds the flight could be seen returning. Algy and Ginger had landed. Biggles waved to them, beckoning urgently. Then he turned again to the Air Commodore. His voice was brittle.

'Will you let me handle this?'

'Yes, but if things go wrong—'

'I know—you'll be held responsible. I'm afraid that's

a risk you'll have to take, sir. I know how many fighters I've got, but how many others are there available on the station? I'm including the two Hurricanes belonging to Crisp and Scrimshaw in my outfit.'

'Apart from those we've seven—all that are left of 910 Squadron.'

'As Crisp isn't back yet, that means we can put up fifteen, all told, if we include my Beaufighter.'

'But are you going to leave the airfield without a single fighter on it?' cried the Air Commodore aghast.

'What are fighters for if not to fight? They'll never have a better opportunity than this, nor is there ever likely to be a greater emergency.'

'But suppose none of them get back?'

'That'll be your worry—I shan't be here,' answered Biggles curtly.

Algy and Ginger came running up. 'What goes on?' asked Algy quickly.

'There's a big formation of Jap bombers on the way,' Biggles told him without emotion. 'We ought to be able to hit them a crack. Algy, I want you to get every fighter on the station lined up—including those Spits that are just landing—with the pilots on parade behind them. Jump to it. Ginger, turn out the squadron. It will line up with the rest. Make it snappy.'

'You're sure you know what you're doing, Bigglesworth?' asked the Air Commodore, in tones of acute anxiety.

'No, I'm not sure,' answered Biggles frankly. 'How can anyone be sure of anything in times like these? I'm hoping, that's all, but that doesn't mean I'm guessing. Sorry I haven't time to talk any more now. See you later.' He walked briskly to where the machines had been mustered in line, with their pilots in a group behind them. He beckoned to Algy. 'Keep those fellows together until I join you; I want a word with them. I shan't be long.'

'Okay.'

Biggles walked on to the end of the line of machines. In a few minutes he was back, facing the line of pilots, officers and sergeants, who were fidgeting at the delay.

'Listen, everyone,' he said loudly. 'You all know what's been going on here—I mean, this secret weapon scare. Forget it. If anyone goes for a Burton to-day it will be from some other cause. Here is your chance to get your own back for what the enemy has done to those messmates who are no longer with us. There are a hundred Japs for you to carve at, so you can help yourselves. There's no escort so it should be a slice of cake. Scrimshaw, last night you seemed to have a load of dirty water on your chest. Now you can get rid of it. My crowd will remember what happened to Angus yesterday.'

'Here comes Johnny Crisp,' said someone.

Looking round Biggles saw Johnny running like a hare across the field.

'Hey! What's going on?' yelled Johnny.

'There's a big Jap formation on the way,' Biggles told him.

'Gimme an aircraft—gimme an aircraft!' bleated Johnny deliriously.

Biggles smiled. 'Sure you're fit to fly?'

'Watch me; oh boy, just watch me!' cried Johnny hysterically.

'All right—take the Beaufighter.' Biggles turned back to the waiting pilots. 'That's all. Give these perishers everything you've got. We haven't far to go. I shall lead in the Typhoon. Let's get weaving.'

There was a rush for the machines.

Biggles started for his aircraft. Pointing eastward, he

shouted to the Air Commodore, who was standing by, 'Get in your car and head up the road that way. You might be in time to see something worth watching.'

The Air Commodore waved understandingly, and ran towards his car.

Biggles climbed into his machine, settled himself in the seat and felt for the throttle. Engines roared, and the mixed formation moved forward, swiftly gaining speed, sending clouds of dust swirling high into the air behind it. Heading eastward, Biggles eased the control column back for altitude.

Five minutes later, at fifteen thousand feet and still climbing, he saw the enemy formation, composed of Mitsubishi bombers as the Air Commodore had stated, strung out like a great dragon across the sky, at an estimated height of twelve thousand feet. He smiled mirthlessly as he altered course a trifle to intercept it. He spoke in the radio.

'Tally-ho, boys! Tally-ho! There they are. We've got 'em. Bertie, get me that leader. Ginger, Tug, stay up to pick off stragglers. Here we go!'

Biggles launched his attack from the starboard quarter, aiming at the neck of the dragon. He went down in a steep dive, with the rest opening out as they streamed down behind him. In an instant the air was being cut into sections by lines of tracer shells and bullets. He picked a Mitsubishi on the near side of the enemy formation, the pilot of which was showing signs of nervousness. Being nearest to the descending tornado he was edging away, forcing others inside the formation to swerve, and lose position in their efforts to avoid collision. To Biggles this was as old as war flying itself. There is usually one such machine in a big formation, and it becomes as much a menace to its own side as to its opponents.

Biggles planned to aggravate the trouble. He held his fire. Tracer flashed past him, but he paid no heed to it, even if he saw it. But when bullets began splashing off his engine cowling he frowned, and pressed a foot gently on the rudder-bar, but without taking his eyes off the bomber he had marked down. He took it in his sights, and at three hundred yards jammed hard on the firing button. The Typhoon shuddered a little as the guns flamed, concentrating a cone of bullets on the Mitsubishi, which swerved wildly, causing others to do the same. The first result of this was not immediately apparent, for the Typhoon had roared over its target to zoom steeply on the other side.

Turning on the top of the zoom Biggles saw that the onset had achieved all that he had hoped of it. The dragon had cracked across the middle, and the formation was now in the shape of a dog's hind leg. Four bombers were going down in different directions and at different angles, one in flames, one smoking. Two others, one of which, Biggles thought, was the swerver, had their wings locked—the prelude to disaster. As he watched they broke apart, one, minus half a wing, to fall spinning. The crew of the other baled out. A Hurricane was also going down, leaving a plume of black smoke to mark its trail. The pilot scrambled out on the fuselage, to be swept off instantly into space by the tearing slipstream.

A look of puzzled astonishment came over Biggles' face as he made out another Hurricane boring along up the middle of the enemy formation blazing a berserk path with its guns. Such madness, far outside the range of recognised tactics, was at all events effective, and the enemy machines were thrown into confusion. But it was also suicidal. Biggles recognised Scrimshaw's machine.

'Scrimshaw, come out of that, you fool,' he snarled into the radio.

Whether Scrimshaw heard the order or not Biggles never knew. He may have tried to obey. At any rate, the Hurricane, all the time under the fire of a dozen enemy gun turrets, whirled round, and then zoomed high. For a moment it hung in a vertical position, its airscrew flashing; then its nose whipped down viciously, dead in line with a Jap. Without altering its course it plunged on, and struck the Mitsubishi just aft of the centre section. There was a blinding explosion, which must have been felt by every aircraft within half a mile. Several other bombers in the immediate vicinity were hurled aside as dead leaves are swept up by a gust of wind. Pieces of the machines that had collided flew far and wide.

'There goes Scrimshaw,' muttered Biggles to himself, as he raced down to plaster the disturbed bombers before their pilots could regain control. At the same time he tried to keep an eye on what was happening. 'Strewth! What a scramble,' he murmured.

The air was now so stiff with milling machines at various altitudes that it was impossible to watch the end of any one incident. It was not easy to avoid collision. The battle resolved itself into a number of fleeting, disjointed impressions. Machines, fighters and bombers, were everywhere, banking, zooming, turning, diving, some unloading bombs. Through this fearful whirlpool bodies were falling, some suspended on parachutes, others dropping sheer. Black, oily smoke, formed ugly streaks against the blue. Only one thing was clear. This big formation had been broken into pieces. It was no longer a cohesive fighting unit. Here and there one or two of the bomber pilots had managed to keep together, and these were being harried by the fighters. Below, bombs were exploding everywhere among the paddy-fields. The smoke of crashed machines rose in mighty pillars. In one place a wood was on fire.

Biggles made no attempt to call off his pack. He realised that no order he could give could make things worse for the bombers. It had to be a fight to the finish. He grabbed a little more altitude to try to get a clearer picture of the entire combat, to see how things were going; at the same time he edged towards the west to cut off any bombers that might still be trying to get through. Ginger and Tug were there—Tug with his undercarriage wheels hanging at a lop-sided angle—circling, sometimes darting in, guns grunting, at bombers that were swerving about in an attempt to get clear of the general mêlée. It was now apparent, however, that although the bombers might have an alternative target, they had given up hope of reaching the original one. In his earphones Biggles could hear Japanese voices. He called Ginger and Tug to him.

'Let's give em what we've got left!' he shouted, knowing that his ammunition, and probably that of the others, was getting low.

In that last wild onslaught he got one bomber for certain, in flames, and two probables. He had a narrow escape. He flinched instinctively as a shower of bombs, flung off by a machine far above him, went sailing past at a curiously oblique angle. A Japanese pilot nearly fell on him, too, as he hurtled earthward with his parachute still packed. Then a sudden reek of glycol told Biggles that his radiator had been damaged, so he turned to the west, calling repeatedly on all pilots to rally.

The surviving bombers were now specks in the sky, most of them heading eastward. The fighters, too, were scattered; on those that were near he focused his eyes, in an endeavour to identify them. He saw Johnny's Beaufighter, looking considerably the worse for wear, limping along on one engine. Other machines, Spitfires and Hurricanes, closed in. In a few minutes, strung out in a line across the sky, they were following.

Biggles' motor packed up just short of the airfield boundary, but he managed to scrape in. Jumping out he watched the Beaufighter circle twice with its under-carriage retracted, and guessed the trouble. Johnny couldn't get his wheels down. At the end of the third circuit, with the ambulance chasing it round, the Beau-fighter made a pancake landing, to finish cocked up on its nose. Biggles smiled when he saw Johnny take a flying leap out of the cockpit and scuttle for a short distance before turning to look at the mess he had made. No one moves faster than an airman leaving an aircraft that is likely to burst into flames. Johnny got a lift on the ambulance, and the driver ran on to pick Biggles up.

'What a party—what a party!' yelled Johnny, who seemed wild with excitement. He appeared to be unaware that his nose was bleeding copiously, the result of his crash landing.

'I think we sort of discouraged them,' said Biggles, grinning.

As they travelled slowly towards the tarmac Biggles checked the machines coming in. He counted eleven. 'Eleven out of sixteen—not bad,' he remarked. Then he saw another machine, flying low, that he had over-looked. 'Twelve,' he corrected.

The station commander was waiting. 'How did it go?' he asked tersely, anxiously.

'We gave them a pasting all right,' answered Biggles. 'Those that are left won't come this way, I'll warrant.

A lot of them unloaded their bombs over the fields, so presumably they'll go back home.'

'How many did you get?'

'I can't tell you that till we've checked up,' replied Biggles. 'We intercepted just this side of the lines, so confirmation ought to be easy, by counting the crashes. The troops on the ground must have had a grandstand view.'

'No trouble with the secret weapon?'

'None at all,' asserted Biggles. 'Excuse me a minute, sir,' he added quickly, 'I'm anxious to find out who's missing. I know Scrimshaw has gone, for one. He either collided with, or deliberately rammed, a Mitsubishi. Something of the sort was pretty certain to happen; he was out for blood.'

The pilots who had landed were now getting out of their machines—all except one. It turned out to be a sergeant pilot of 910 Squadron with a bullet through his shoulder. An ambulance rushed him to hospital.

A quick check revealed that the missing pilots were Ginger, Henry Harcourt, Scrimshaw, and a pilot officer of 910 Squadron. One or two of those that returned had received minor wounds. All the machines showed signs of punishment. Bertie had had a remarkable escape. A cannon shell entering through the side of the cockpit had torn the sole off his boot without touching the foot, and then remained transfixed near the root of the control column without exploding.

'Did anybody see what happened to Ginger?' asked Biggles sharply. 'I was with him just before the finish. He seemed all right then.'

Nobody answered. Apparently nobody had seen Ginger go down.

'He may have baled out,' said Biggles. 'That goes for all of them—except Scrimshaw. He went for a

Burton in a big way.'

'I'm not sure, but I fancy Henry got it in the first dive,' put in Tex. 'I didn't see him after that, but I noticed a machine going down, and it looked like his.'

'Well, we shall have to wait.' Biggles turned to the Group Captain. 'Where's the Air Commodore?'

'He went off up the road and hasn't come back yet,' answered the Group Captain. 'Good show, you fellows. That's a load off my mind, I can tell you. I wonder why the Japs didn't use their secret weapon?'

'There was probably a reason,' remarked Biggles softly. 'This looks like the Air Commodore coming now. He's got someone with him. Who is it?'

'It's Henry,' said Algy, as the car drew nearer.

The car did not stop, but raced on to the medical hut.

'That means Henry's hurt,' observed Biggles. 'Phew! Is it hot, and am I dry! Let's go and get a drink.'

Before they reached the mess the Air Commodore joined them. He was smiling. 'Great show, Bigglesworth—absolutely terrific,' he complimented. 'I never saw such a scramble. At one moment I counted five Mitsubishis all falling at once.'

'What about Henry?' asked Biggles.

'Nothing very serious, but I'm afraid he'll be off your strength for a bit. One of the bullets that set his machine alight slashed his arm badly. He baled out, but hit a tree and damaged his leg. I fancy it's broken.'

Biggles lit a cigarette. 'Bad luck. Did you see anything of Ginger?'

'Oh, dear! Isn't he back? No, I didn't see him. That's not surprising, though. Machines were falling all over the sky. There is this about it though; if he baled out he'll be on our side of the lines.'

Biggles nodded. 'How many bombers do you reckon

we got? We haven't checked up yet.'

'I counted twenty-three hit the ground, but there must be a lot of others that won't get back. I noticed several making off, shedding bits and pieces, and they've a long way to go over that forest to their nearest airfield. Funny there was no sign of the secret weapon.'

'Very odd,' agreed Biggles, smiling faintly. 'I'm going in for a drink—I'm as dry as an old boot. I want a word with you later, sir, but I shall have to see about combat reports first, while the thing is fresh in everyone's mind. You might send someone up to the lines to ask the troops if they saw where our machines fell. It's not much use looking for them from the air, with all that mess about, unless we have some definite information to go on. You'd better arrange for a party to go out and collect the loose Japs, too; I saw a lot of them bale out.'

'I'll do that,' promised the Air Commodore. 'See you presently.'

Followed by the others Biggles walked on to the mess.

Chapter 11
Biggles Sums Up

It was shortly after lunch when Air Commodore Raymond walked into the ante-room, to find the officers of 666 Squadron sitting about, or reclining, for it was the hottest time of the day and the heat was intense. Conversation still centred on the morning's big dogfight, concerning which fresh details were being remembered and narrated, some humorous, some tragic.

'Any news of Ginger, sir?' asked Biggles, when the Air Commodore entered, and the others gathered round him.

'Not a word. By the way, have you heard how Mackail is getting on?'

'I rang up the hospital about half an hour ago,' returned Biggles. 'He's about the same—certainly no worse. I'm more worried about Ginger at the moment.'

'All units near the line are being questioned,' stated the Air Commodore. 'So many machines came down in a small area that it's hard to trace any particular one. How many bombers do you reckon you got, now you've made a check?'

'We make it twenty-six certain, ten probables, and at least thirty damaged.'

The Air Commodore smiled. 'Your fellows are too modest. There are thirty-one down on our side alone; several others were observed to be losing height as they made for home.'

Biggles nodded. 'Good. If we don't hear something about Ginger pretty soon we'll take what machines are serviceable and try to locate his aircraft. Has the M.O. made his report yet about Sergeant Gray?'

'Yes.'

'What has he to say about him?'

'He's a bit puzzled, because the state of the body presents some unusual features; but he can't find anything to account for death, which he has ascribed to heart failure. The strange thing is, he says Gray had not been drinking.'

'I could have told him that,' murmured Biggles. 'No sign of poison?'

'None. Nor were there any signs of a self-inflicted wound.'

'There wouldn't be,' said Biggles grimly.

'Why not?'

'Because Gray was murdered.'

The Air Commodore stared. 'Are you serious?'

'This isn't exactly an occasion for mirth.'

'You speak as though you are certain Gray was murdered.'

'I'm convinced of it—now.'

'But who on earth would kill Gray?'

'We've already discussed this, you remember? Any enemy agent would kill him. He was killed to prevent him from talking. I think I know who did it, but I'd rather not mention names until I have proof. I hope to have that very soon.'

'You astound me,' said the Air Commodore, looking shaken. 'You haven't wasted your time.'

'I've none to waste—life is too short. Besides which, India in the hot season isn't my idea of heaven. I want to get this job tied up so that I can go home.'

'What about the secret weapon? From the way you behaved when you took off to intercept the Jap formation I gathered you had an idea about it.'

119

'I've more than an idea,' answered Biggles. 'I know what it is. Only it isn't a weapon. I'd call it a trick.'

The Air Commodore looked thunderstruck. 'Are you telling me that—you have—actually got to the bottom of the thing?'

'Let us say almost. I'm far enough into it to see the bottom, anyway.'

'But this is wonderful!' cried the Air Commodore. 'I'll tell the Air Marshal that we've got the thing buttoned up.'

'I didn't say that,' disputed Biggles. 'Let's put it like this. When I tackled the job it seemed to me that there were two angles to it. The first was to find the thing, and learn how it did the mischief; the second was to put a stop to it. The first part has been done, but the second part is still very much in the air. We've got to be careful. If once the enemy realises that we've rumbled his game he'll slide away like a ghost on roller skates, maybe to start again somewhere else with a variation of the racket. We've got to bait the hook and strike our fish before he realises that we're after him. As it is, I'm a bit worried that he'll smell a rat.'

'Why?'

'Because of what happened this morning. He'll know how many machines we put up, and how many came back. In other words, he'll know that for once his secret weapon went off at half-cock. True, he may think that was partly due to luck, or to the fact that it was a short show. That's what I'm hoping. But he *may* guess the truth. It is even possible that he saw me spike his guns, so to speak.'

'You actually did that?'

'On this very airfield—right in front of your eyes.'

The Air Commodore looked at Biggles suspiciously. 'Are you pulling my leg?'

'Have a heart, sir. What have I ever done to create the impression that I'm an irresponsible humorist?'

'Where is this weapon?'

'In my pocket. Would you like to see it?'

'I certainly would.'

In dead silence Biggles put his hand in his pocket and produced a small bar of chocolate. 'That's it.'

No one spoke. In an embarrassing silence the Air Commodore looked at the chocolate, then at Biggles, whose face was expressionless. 'Are you out of your mind?' he asked coldly.

'You would be, if you browsed for a little while on this particular sample of confectionery.'

Understanding began to dawn in the Air Commodore's eyes. A mutter of amazement came from the assembled officers.

The Air Commodore's eyes came to rest on Biggles' face. 'Would you mind explaining?'

'I'm going to tell you the whole story, so far as I know it,' returned Biggles. 'I think it is my duty to do so, although the tale is not yet complete. In this detective line of business it was the practice of that prince of sleuths, Sherlock Holmes, to keep his clues and whatnots under his hat until he had the whole thing nicely rounded off, and then explode the solution with a rousing bang under the startled noses of his baffled associates. That technique, I regret to observe, has been maintained by the more humble members of his profession who have followed him. I say I regret it because it's stupid, it's selfish, and for all practical reasons, pointless. Had Holmes been knocked down by a cab, or otherwise accidentally been sent for a Burton, his secret, the result of his investigations, would have gone west with him, and the villains would have got away with it after all. In our case I'm not going to risk that happening. If the skunk who is operating on this airfield didn't mind killing Gray, he would, if he knew I was after him, be delighted to stick a knife in my ribs. In case that should happen you will be able to carry on, so here's the gen as far as I've got. It's a bit of a mouthful, but by the time I've finished you'll know exactly what's been happening and how things stand right now. Taffy, go over to that door and don't let anyone come near it. Tex—Ferocity, you take the windows and do the same thing. Sorry to be dramatic, but I'm not taking any chances of being overheard. The rest of you make yourselves comfortable. We've got the afternoon in front of us, and it's too hot to do anything, anyway. Moreover, I'm not quite ready for the next move. This is the story, so far.' Biggles sank into an easy chair and lit a cigarette.

'The first thing that struck me about this weapon was that the Japs had invented it,' he began. 'The Japanese don't invent things—at least, not mechanical devices. They're good at copying other people's. They'll copy anything—they even copied their language from China. It would be a strange thing, you must admit, if they had produced a mechanical device, like a death ray, for instance, that has baffled Western scientists. For this reason I worked on the assumption that the hidden death was not a mechanical instrument. The next outstanding feature was the peculiar inconstancy of this alleged weapon. The machines on the China run that did get through, got through without any interference. Why? If this weapon was as efficient as it appeared to be on one occasion, why should it fail utterly on the next? The locality of the aircraft, the weather conditions, in fact, all conditions, were precisely the same. Yet obviously something was different. What could it be? There was another factor, a curious one, but to me, significant. Only machines flying from west to east were lost. Machines flying from Chungking to India got through. Again, why? A ray, or beam, or any other weapon, would surely work the same whichever way the aircraft was travelling. One was forced to the conclusion that whatever was happening was the result of something that started on the ground, not in the air. Clearly, the thing did not start at Chungking. There was no intermediate landing-ground, so it looked as if the trouble was at Jangpur. And whatever was happening there was happening, broadly speaking, to the aircraft.

'Now, an aircraft in flight consists of three parts— the airframe, the motor, and the pilot. The failure of any of these must result in the failure of the whole. Therefore, should any one of these be affected the result would be the same—the machine would not get through. The question was, which was it? I resolved to tackle the three things separately, in turn. Frankly, I suspected that either the airframe, the engine, or the pilot, was being sabotaged—and in the end I was not far out. It was, I suppose, a natural assumption—the first thing that would strike anybody. The problem was to find out *what* was being sabotaged, and how.

'I could think of no other way of testing this than by actual practice, so I decided to fly from Jangpur to Chungking. It was not what you'd call a fascinating experiment, because I like living as much as anybody, and I was staking my life against an opinion. I made the trip, taking Bargent, the original pilot, with me. Nothing happened. Why didn't anything happen? The answer, according to my line of surmise, wasn't hard to find. Nothing happened because until I climbed into the aircraft no one, except Frayle, the C.O., Bargent, and myself, knew that particular machine was going to make the run. I took precautions to make sure nobody knew. In any case, the decision was taken so suddenly that there could have been no time for anyone to interfere with the machine. Another aircraft had been detailed, and I'm pretty certain that had I flown it, it would not have got through. Anyhow, there was lesson number one. I had proved that an unexpected pilot flying an unexpected aircraft could get through. This was in accord with my theory, and the implication was obvious. A saboteur was at work at Jangpur, a man who was in a position to know which machine was next on the schedule to make the run. It seemed safe to assume that what was happening at Jangpur was also happening here. I didn't risk a second trip at Jangpur. Oh, no. It might not have come off a second time.' Biggles lit another cigarette.

'So for my second experiment I came here,' he continued. 'It confirmed my opinion. Officially, we are a communication squadron, so nobody—I mean the saboteur—would expect our Mosquito to suddenly take off and head for Burma. Again I got away with it—for that very reason. Angus' arrival on the scene was not in my programme. He came up the river on his own account. But mark this! I understand there was some discussion in the mess as to who was going to escort Tug. This must have been overheard by the saboteur, who had time to sabotage Angus' machine before it took off. All this was supporting my theory.'

'But Tug Carrington went back up the river,' reminded the Air Commodore. 'Why was his machine not tampered with?'

'For the very obvious reason that he did not take a machine from this station. He flew a seaplane, and had to go some distance to get it. The saboteur, even if he knew about it, would have no time to get to it.'

'Of course, I'd overlooked that,' said the Air Commodore.

'Sergeant Gray, poor fellow, unwittingly provided the next link in the chain,' resumed Biggles. 'And a startling one it was. I told you that when I landed in the forest beside Moorven's crash I found nothing. That was not strictly true. I did find something, but at the time it suggested no sinister purpose. In fact, I threw it away and thought no more of it. It was a little square of pink paper, bearing the name of a British confectionery manufacturer. When I found just such a piece in A Flight shed, when Sergeant Gray was there, drunk, as we thought, I began to wonder. There was something else in that room that aroused my suspicions. It was a coffee-pot. On the occasion of my first visit I sent for coffee. Gray drank it all.

'When I went back, hours later, the coffee-pot was still warm. I could find only one explanation of that. Somebody had been to Gray with a fresh pot of coffee. Gray was hardly in a state to fetch it. Had he wanted it, it is far more likely that he would have gone across to the canteen. The person who took that coffee, took it because he wanted an excuse for going there, in case he was seen. He had good reason for caution. He went to kill Gray, for fear Gray would talk. Gray, had he lived, would have insisted that he was not drunk. He could have proved it. This would have led to the question, were the other cases of drunkenness on the station—there had been some, you know—really that, or were the men the victims of a mysterious malady? The saboteur did not want that sort of talk, we may be sure. With one thing and another I began to get a glimmering of the truth. You see, after Johnny told me that on the day Moorven was killed they had swopped planes, I suspected that it was the pilot, not the aircraft, that was being tampered with.

'Now let me come to my first flight of this morning. I set a trap. In the mess I briefed two machines and two pilots to go out over Burma—Ginger and Johnny. I said nothing about going myself, although I intended going.' Biggles paused to smile. 'I wanted the saboteur to work on the other two machines, but not on mine. Actually, there was very little risk, because I had not the slightest intention of letting Johnny and Ginger go anywhere near Burma, nor, for that matter, be in the air long enough for the secret weapon to work. We landed at Gayhar, and sat there on the ground with our engines running. Things did not pan out as I expected them to, and I don't mind admitting that I got a shock when Johnny passed out. I thought it would be Ginger. Bearing Sergeant Gray in mind I was prepared to find one of them in a state *resembling* drunkenness, but actually in a condition of coma, the result of being drugged.'

'Hey! I like that,' cried Johnny. 'How did you know we weren't going to be poisoned?'

Biggles laughed at Johnny's indignation. 'Had the stuff been poison it would not have been necessary to murder Sergeant Gray, would it? No, he would have died anyway. I was pretty sure that the stuff was a powerful narcotic rather than a poison. There were strong arguments against the use of poison, as I shall presently explain. I had worked it out, from the discovery of the pink paper, that the dope was being administered in chewing-gum, which would occasion no surprise if it were found in an aircraft. It would be a simple matter to get the stuff into machines briefed for flights over enemy country. Judge my chagrin and alarm when Johnny, after we brought him round, swore that he had not touched any chewing-gum. Nor, in fact, was there any in his machine. I was flabbergasted. It looked as if I was wrong. But when I inspected Johnny's machine, and found on the floor the wrapping of a bar of chocolate, I knew I was right. This wrapping-paper, I may say, bore the same name as that on the chewing-gum wrapping—Charneys, London. Only the method had been changed. Chocolate was now being used instead of gum. I found a piece of the same brand of chocolate in Ginger's machine; as it happened, he hadn't touched it. If he had, he would have passed out, too. If Johnny had had a grain of common sense he would have told me that he had eaten chocolate.'

'I like that,' protested Johnny vehemently. 'I'm not a thought reader. You were talking about chewing-gum.'

'It's all confectionery,' declared Biggles. 'The next question was, why had the saboteur suddenly switched from gum to chocolate? That puzzled me for a little while. Then I hit on what I think is a reasonable explanation. The saboteur had realised that Johnny always got back *because he didn't like chewing-gum*, so to get him he baited his machine with chocolate. And he got him. Had Johnny gone out over Burma in that machine he wouldn't be here now.'

'But what about your machine, old boy?' put in Bertie. 'Wasn't there any chocolate or chewing-gum in that?'

'No.'

'Why not?'

'Because, my poor chump, I gave no indication that I was going on the sortie. The only person who knew I was going, was me. I took good care of that. Supposing that I was staying on the ground, the dope merchant did not bait my machine. Only machines briefed for operations received that sort of attention, otherwise the wrong people might have got hold of the bait, with awkward consequences. That, of course, is what happened to Sergeant Gray. Johnny never touches gum. A week ago he came back with a piece of gum still in the pocket of the aircraft where it had been planted. Gray, looking over the machine, as he was bound to, found it. He chewed it, and passed out. Everyone thought he was drunk. He wasn't. He was doped. The same thing happened yesterday. I would wager that when Johnny came back from the sortie when Moorven and the others were lost, he had a piece of chewing-gum on board. Am I right, Johnny?'

'Now you mention it I recall seeing a packet.'

'Exactly. Gray found it. The same performance was repeated. Dash it, poor Gray almost *told* us what had happened. He said he had been sitting there *chewing* the thing over, but no one took him literally. He became unconscious. It was known that we were waiting for him to come round to ask him questions. That hadn't happened on the previous occasion. It was realised that he might mention the chewing-gum to us. So he was quietly murdered. We now know why Johnny and Scrimshaw always came back. Neither of them touched chewing-gum.'

'What a devilish scheme,' muttered the Air Commodore.

'But horribly effective,' returned Biggles. 'What has been happening is now plain enough. A pilot takes off. Sooner or later he discovers a piece of chewing-gum in the aircraft. He chews it. The narcotic takes effect. By that time it is too late for him to do anything about it. Johnny has told me how everything suddenly swam before his eyes. He lost the use of his limbs. The machine falls, crashes, and the pilot is killed. Very simple, but as I just said effective. The mysterious interval of time between the falling out of the machines is now explained. Naturally, the time when a machine went down would depend on when the pilot found the dope. Yesterday, three pilots died like that. Moorven was the first to find the gum. He was the first to fall. After he had put a piece of the stuff in his mouth he dropped the wrapping paper on the floor, where I found it.'

'Frightful,' muttered the Air Commodore.

Biggles went on: 'To some people, this putting stuff in the cockpit of an aircraft might seem a haphazard sort of scheme. Actually, it was more likely to succeed in its purpose than a bomb. One would notice a bomb—but not a piece of chewing-gum. The more you think about it the more devilishly cunning it appears. Nothing could look more natural than gum, nothing more harmless. Scores of pilots chew gum regularly when in the air; we've all done it and we've all left odd packets in our machines. On a long flight a fellow would be almost certain to find the stuff: and having found it, ninety-nine out of a hundred would sample a piece. Of course, there would be occasional exceptions, like Johnny and Scrimshaw. I'm sorry about Scrimshaw. In his fury he lost his head—practically threw his life away. Yet even the exceptions like Johnny and Scrimshaw wouldn't escape indefinitely. As we have seen, chocolate could be substituted for gum. If it turned out they didn't like chocolate, no doubt in course of time they would have been tempted with biscuits, popcorns, or acid drops. Sooner or later their turn would have come.'

'A grim thought,' put in the Air Commodore.

Biggles continued: 'The devilish scheme had one big snag. Once put into action, it could not be allowed to fail. Had the dope got into wrong hands people would have started falling about all over the airfield, and the game would have been up. There is no doubt that this did happen once or twice. When I first arrived I was told that there had been several cases of drunkenness. These men weren't drunk; like Gray, they were doped; but who was to guess it? But too much of that sort of thing would have led to questions. We can see why dope was used instead of poison. Had these men, who were supposed to be drunk, died, there would have been trouble. That would have meant an investigation and the scheme might have been discovered. The after-effects of a narcotic are not unlike those of alcohol—which is, in fact, a narcotic.'

'Do you know what drug they are using?' asked the Air Commodore.

'Not yet. It doesn't matter much, does it? The East is rotten with drugs—opium, hashish, bhang, charas, qhat, and heaven only knows what else. The next problem is to find the devil who dishes out the stuff.'

At this point Taffy, who was still at the door, let out a yell. 'Here comes Ginger, look you!' he shouted. 'By Davy! Is he in a mess!'

A moment later Ginger appeared in the doorway. He was hatless, perspiring freely, mud-plastered from head to foot with a layer of grey dust over the mud. But he was smiling.

'What cheer, everybody,' he greeted, and then flopped on the nearest settee. 'Blimey! What a climate . . . what a country,' he murmured with intense feeling.

Chapter 12
The Oriental Touch

Ginger was welcomed with boisterous enthusiasm.

'Where have you been all this time?' demanded Biggles, when the babble had abated.

'Walking, mostly,' was the weary reply. 'I've walked miles and miles and miles. Eventually I got a lift on a bullock cart to a road, where I was lucky enough to be picked up by a jeep on the way to Calcutta.'

'What happened to you?'

'Nothing astonishing.' Ginger made a gesture of chagrin. 'I blotted my copy book,' he confessed. 'I got a brace of bombers and went out for the hat trick. One of my little ambitions has always been to get three birds with one stone, so to speak. Unfortunately I hadn't much ammo left, so to make sure I went in close.' Ginger smiled lugubriously. 'I went too close. I thought the rear gunner was looking the other way, but he couldn't have been. As soon as I opened up he handed me a squirt that nearly knocked my engine off its bearers. I had to bale out.'

'Did you get *him*?' demanded Ferocity.

Ginger shook his head sadly. 'That's the irritating part of it. I don't know. I couldn't hang around long enough to see.'

There was a titter of mirth.

'I got down all right—in the middle of a thousand acre paddy-field. The rice was growing in mud. I never want to see rice again. That's all. What's going on here—a mother's meeting?'

'Not exactly,' returned Biggles. 'Go and have a clean up and you'll be in time for tea.'

'I suppose I might as well,' murmured Ginger, rising. 'What a life.'

After he had gone the debate was resumed.

'We must get on with this,' averred the Air Commodore. 'I'm anxious to hear the rest. When Ginger came in you were saying something about the enemy agent who has been, and presumably still is, working here. You had previously said you thought you knew who it was. Whom do you suspect?'

'The genial Lal Din.'

'That moon-faced steward!' The Air Commodore looked incredulous.

'Yes.'

'But he has no business near the machines.'

'He may have no business, but as he is so well known it is doubtful if anyone would comment if he was seen strolling round. From what Johnny tells me it seems—ironically enough—that the culprit handed the stuff to Sergeant Gray to put in the machines. Very cute. Gray, of course, had no idea what he was doing. Lal Din—or whoever it is—would probably pass it over with a remark to the effect that the stuff was a regulation issue, or a free issue, from the people at home. Such a statement would not be questioned. It becomes still plainer to see why Sergeant Gray had to be silenced. Had we been allowed to question him it would have emerged that the only thing that passed his lips was chewing-gum. He would have remembered where he got it, how it got into the plane, and who gave it to him.'

'If we keep watch, we ought to be able to catch the scoundrel red-handed,' suggested the Air Commodore.

'If we keep watch,' argued Biggles, 'we shall be more

likely to start the whole station talking. One word, and our dope merchant will take fright. I'm pretty sure it's Lal Din. He's not what he says he is, anyway. He tries to make out he's a Burmese Chinaman, and he talks English like one—up to a point. But his accent is a bit *too* pronounced for a man who has lived his life in Burma, and has been in British service. I'd say he's got Jap blood in him. Anyway, I started working this morning on the assumption that Lal Din was an enemy agent. I made sure he was present when I briefed the flight in the mess, by ordering a packet of cigarettes. He stood by with them on his tray while I was giving my orders. So at any rate he knew, or thought he knew, which machines were going out. I deliberately gave him time to do his dirty work. The same sort of thing must have happened before. As a mess waiter Lal Din would hear talk, and perhaps see Daily Orders on the notice-board. He was in this mess when Angus asked Algy's permission to escort Tug, when Tug was coming to fetch me in the seaplane. Incidentally, it may interest you to know that nearly all the machines which took off this morning to intercept the Jap formation were planted with dope—including the Spitfires I asked you to recall. I went to each aircraft before the sortie and collected the stuff. That's what I meant when I said I'd spiked the secret weapon under your nose.'

'I wondered what you were doing, dashing from plane to plane,' put in the Air Commodore.

'Now you will understand, too, what I meant when I spoke of the saboteur smelling a rat. It would probably be easier to get the dope put in the aircraft than recover it from them when they came back. He's probably puzzled as to why so many of our machines *did* come back. He'll be still more puzzled if he ascertains that the doped confectionery was apparently eaten—or at any rate, discovers that it has disappeared. We must be careful that he does not learn the truth. It was for that reason that I did not take the rather obvious course of putting a guard on the machines after they returned. This saboteur, whoever he is, is cunning, and once he spotted that the machines were being watched, not only would he keep clear, but he might fade away altogether. There are other ways of discovering who he is. I prefer to give him enough rope to hang himself—and other people. Assuming that the operative on this airfield is Lal Din, it doesn't follow that he is the instigator of the scheme, or that he is working alone. It is more likely that there is a big organization behind him. Similar men are on the same job at Jangpur, Ceylon, and elsewhere. We don't know who they are. We must find out before we can hope to rope in the whole network. When we strike we've got to make a clean sweep and pull in the brains behind the show. We've got to find out how the dope is getting into the confectionery. We can be quite sure that it doesn't come out from England like that. Charneys, the manufacturers, are a big, old-established British firm, quite above suspicion. Clearly, someone is getting hold of the stuff at this end and putting the dope into it. Not all of it, of course; but a certain quantity which is kept handy for use as required. Someone has access to this stuff when it arrives from England. He must be found, otherwise, if it becomes known that the chewing-gum and chocolate racket has been rumbled, we may have all sorts of foodstuffs being doped. That would mean scrapping thousands of tons of perfectly good food which would become suspect.'

'Yes—er—quite so,' said the Air Commodore, in a strange voice.

Biggles looked at him questioningly. 'Is something

the matter?'

'No.' Raymond smiled—a funny, twisted smile. 'You've shaken me to the marrow, that's all. Not so much by the nature of this thing as by the way you've rooted it out.'

'We haven't finished yet,' declared Biggles, shaking his head. 'We're only half-way. Before we make our next move there will have to be some careful planning. The first question to arise is, what are we going to do about the other stations that are affected? Of course, it would be the easiest thing in the world to get in touch with the commanders of those stations and tell them to order their pilots to lay off the confectionery. But if we did that it's a dead cert that the enemy would hear about it. A safer plan would be to keep all machines grounded—except in case of dire emergency—for the time being. If we aren't ready to strike in twenty-four hours then I'm afraid we shall have to let the other stations know what is causing the trouble. But give me a few hours before you do that.'

'It seems to me,' said the Air Commodore, 'that the first thing we've got to do is to establish beyond all doubt that Lal Din is our man.'

'And then what?'

'We'll arrest him and make him talk.'

'Suppose he doesn't talk? We shall have stumped ourselves. Remember, if he's what we think he is, he's our only link with the enemy organization.'

'But I'm thinking about the urgency of the matter,' returned the Air Commodore. 'If it turned out that he was our man, and could be made to tell us the name of his employer, we could strike immediately and clear the whole thing up.'

Biggles shook his head. 'It's risky. Of course, if it came off it would be fine, but if it failed we should be worse off than before.'

'I think it's worth taking a chance,' decided the Air Commodore. 'Could you devise a means of finding out right away if Lal Din is the culprit?'

'That should be easy,' replied Biggles. He shrugged. 'We'll try it if you like, but if it fails, don't blame me.'

'Try it,' advised the Air Commodore.

'All right,' agreed Biggles, without enthusiasm. 'Algy, go to the 'phone, ring up the central canteen, and ask the manager to send Lal Din over here with some cigarettes.'

Algy went to the 'phone.

'When Lal Din comes in, you fellows at the door and windows keep on your toes in case, when he realises that the game is up, he tries to make a break,' ordered Biggles.

Presently Lal Din came, beaming as usual. 'Cigarettes?' said he, looking round the room.

Biggles, from the easy chair in which he was seated, put up a hand. 'Over here.'

Still beaming, Lal Din approached, and handed over the cigarettes. He was turning away when Biggles called him back.

'By the way, Lal Din,' he said, 'do you like chocolate?'

The Oriental did not start. His walk seemed to freeze to a standstill. He looked back over his shoulder—still beaming.

Biggles tossed a bar of chocolate on a small table in front of him. 'Try that,' he suggested.

Lal Din did not move. His broad smile became fixed, the humour gone out of it. The atmosphere in the room was electric.

'What's the matter?' said Biggles evenly. 'Don't you like chocolate?'

Very slowly the steward reached out and picked up the bar. 'Me eat after work,' he said.

'Eat it now,' ordered Biggles. He spoke quietly, but there was an edge to his voice.

The steward did not move. His eyes were fixed on Biggles' face, as if he would read what was going on behind the impassive countenance.

'Eat it,' snapped Biggles.

Very slowly the steward looked round the circle of faces. Then, like an automaton actuated by a hidden spring, he moved. He streaked to the far side of the room, and as he ran he drew from somewhere a small narrow-bladed knife. In front of the fireplace he dropped on his knees.

Biggles was on his feet. 'Stop him!' he shouted.

But he was too late. With a calm, but swift deliberation that was horrible to watch, the steward drove the blade into his side, and dragged it across his stomach. Gasping, he fell forward on his face.

The breathless hush that followed was broken by Biggles. 'Call the ambulance, somebody,' he said bitterly. 'Let's get him out of this.' He looked at the Air Commodore. 'That should settle any doubts about his nationality. Only a Japanese would commit hara-kari. Well, there goes our link with the enemy organization. We might have guessed he'd do something like that when he saw the game was up—and he knew it was up the instant he saw that chocolate. That would tell him why the big blitz failed this morning, and why so many of us got back. He'd never dare to tell his boss that he'd failed. That would mean losing face, which is worse than death to a Japanese. So he took a short cut to eternity. Pity, but there it is. One can't be right all the time.'

Chapter 13
Fresh Plans

The ambulance came, and went, taking the body of the treacherous steward. Also the bloodstained hearth-rug.

'Yes, it's a pity about that,' said the Air Commodore uneasily. 'It was my fault. I should have left you alone.'

'We found out what we wanted to know and a fat lot of good it has done us,' replied Biggles moodily. 'But there, the damage is done, and it's no use moaning about it. We tried a scheme that might have saved us a lot of trouble. It didn't work. Now we must think of something else.'

'I'd better leave you to it,' murmured the Air Commodore contritely. 'When I butt in I do more harm than good. You've done marvellously, Bigglesworth. Keep it going.' He went out.

Biggles dropped into a chair.

'That was a dirty business.' remarked Algy.

'It was really my fault. I should have insisted on playing the game my own way. Still, let's be charitable. Raymond is nearly out of his mind with worry; he must be desperately anxious to get the business buttoned up.'

'What are you going to do next?' asked Algy. 'Is there anything you can do?'

'Oh, yes.' answered Biggles readily. 'There are plenty of things; the question is, which is the best? We've no time to lose. As it is, I'm scared that the return of nearly all our machines this morning will have made the whole enemy organization suspicious.

Now, on top of that, comes this business of Lal Din slicing himself in halves. When his boss hears about that—'

'But will he?' interposed Algy.

'If he doesn't hear about it he'll soon know that Lal Din is no longer here; or if he is, that he is not on the job.'

'I don't see why he should know.'

'Of course he will. Look at it this way. What will be the reaction of the chief enemy agent in India to the wiping out of the big Jap formation this morning, followed by the return of nearly all our machines? The first thing he'll do is try to get in touch with Lal Din, the man on the spot, to demand an explanation.'

'Yes, I think that's a reasonable assumption,' agreed Algy.

'He will then discover that Lal Din isn't available, and you can bet your life it won't take him long to find out why. That's why we've got to move fast.' Biggles thought for amoment. 'I'll tell you what. Let's go to the canteen to find out if anyone has already been making inquiries about Lal Din. I think it's an angle worth watching. Did you get that list of personnel I wanted?'

'Yes.'

'Who's the manager of the canteen?'

Algy took a sheet of paper from his pocket and ran an eye over it. 'Ali Mansur,' he answered. 'He's an ex-Askari, a retired sergeant of the King's African Rifles— twenty-four years' service. Got the D.C.M.* and the Long Service Medal.'

'That should put him above suspicion, anyway,' declared Biggles. 'Let's go and see him.'

---

* Distinguished Conduct Medal

They found the manager in his office. He was an elderly, dark-skinned, heavily moustached man, with a soldierly bearing, wearing his medal ribbons on the lapel of a spotless white jacket. He had not yet learned of the fate of his assistant, and after dwelling for a moment or two on the need for secrecy, Biggles told him the truth, which in any case could not long be concealed—that Lal Din was dead by his own hand.

'This man was a Japanese spy,' said Biggles. 'He could not face defeat. The chief Japanese secret agent will soon want an explanation of the decisive blow we struck this morning against the enemy bombers. What I am anxious to know, sergeant, is this. Has anyone been here making inquiries for Lal Din?'

'Not today, sahib,' replied the sergeant.

'You're sure of that?'

'If such a one had been here I should know of it.'

'Has Lal Din been out, or asked for time off?'

'No, sahib. He could not leave the station without my permission.'

'What exactly did you mean when you said, not today? Have inquiries been made for him on other occasions?'

'Yes, sahib.'

'By whom?'

'His brother, or a man calling himself a brother, comes to see him.'

'Have you seen this brother?'

'No, sahib.'

'How's that?'

'I rarely leave the station, and the brother has no permit to enter. So we have not met.'

'What happens, then?'

'The brother, or any stranger, must go to the main gate. There he speaks to the N.C.O. of the guard, asking for Lal Din. The N.C.O. rings me on the telephone, and if it is possible I allow Lal Din to go to the gate. You must understand, though, that there were days when Lal Din took time off. Then, doubtless, he left the station, although where he went I do not know. I can only tell you of what happens when the brother comes asking for him when he is on duty.'

'This has sometimes happened?'

'Often, sahib.'

'But it has not happened today?'

'No, sahib.'

'Thank you, sergeant. You have told me just what I wanted to know.' Biggles turned to Algy. 'We're lucky. No one has been here yet, but in view of what happened in the air this morning I think someone *will* call. Of course, it may be that the chief saboteur is waiting for Lal Din to report to him with an explanation. When he doesn't show up someone will be sent to find out why. That may take time. I can't afford to wait. I've another line of approach up my sleeve, and I'd like to tackle it right away.' Biggles turned back to Sergeant Mansur. 'There is another matter I would like to discuss with you. Who gave Lal Din his job at this station?'

'I did, sahib. As mess caterer I employ my own staff—with the approval of the adjutant*, of course.'

'How did you get in touch with Lal Din?'

'There was a vacancy, sahib, and he came to me on a recommendation.'

'From whom?'

'Messrs. Tahil and Larapindi.'

'Who are they?'

---

* An officer specially appointed to assist the commanding officer with all official correspondence and administrative duties.

'Shippers' and merchants' agents, sahib. They represent many British firms in India. Much goods imported go through their hands. They have a big warehouse at the docks, in Calcutta, and offices in many Eastern towns.'

'Does this firm supply stuff to our canteen?'

'Yes, sahib.'

'Things like chocolate, chewing-gum . . .'

'Yes, among other things, sahib.'

'When is this stuff delivered, and how?'

'When we need supplies I ring up Tahil and Larapindi, and they send the goods up in one of their cars.'

'And what happens when the stuff gets here?'

'It is unloaded and put out for sale.'

'Who unloads it?'

'Sometimes I check it in, sahib; sometimes Lal Din, or one of the other assistants, might do it.'

'Anyway, the stuff is taken to the canteen and made available for the troops?'

'Yes, sahib.'

'And this firm recommended Lal Din?'

'Not the firm exactly, sahib. Mr. Larapindi rang me up on the telephone and asked me to find work for a very good man he knew.'

'I see,' said Biggles slowly. 'What sort of man is this Larapindi—have you seen him?'

'Many times, sahib. He is Eurasian, but of what precise nationality I do not know. He is a small man, with a brown face, and wears very large spectacles.'

'I am told there has been a free issue of chocolate and chewing-gum. Is that so?'

'Yes, sahib.'

'How long has it been going on?'

'It is not a regular thing. We had the first case sent up not long ago. It came with other goods from Tahil and Larapindi.'

'Was this after Lal Din arrived?'

'Yes, sahib.'

'And he dished the stuff out?'

'Yes, sahib—he offered to do it.'

'Thank you, sergeant. You have been most helpful.' Biggles turned to Algy. 'This is worth following up.' he said quietly. 'I've half a mind to abandon my alternative scheme, which was to slip up to Jangpur to try to nab the fellow there who is doing what Lal Din was doing here. If I could get my hands on him I might make him speak.'

At this moment Air Commodore Raymond came hurrying into the canteen. 'I've been looking everywhere for you,' he told Biggles.

'Now what's wrong, sir?' queried Biggles.

'The Higher Command says we simply must get this China route in full operation again. The Chinese doctors are having to perform operations on their wounded without anaesthetics. Not only are medical stores urgently needed, but several senior officials are waiting to go through. Now we know what caused the trouble I thought perhaps you could do something about it, if it isn't upsetting your plans.'

'No. As a matter of fact it fits in with my plans quite well,' returned Biggles. You can reckon that the route will be functioning again to-morrow. I'll slip up right away to see Frayle. All you have to do is send him some machines, and pilots to fly them.'

'And you don't think there will be any more risk?'

'I don't think so, sir—at any rate, not if my plan succeeds.'

'Then I can tell the A.O.C. that the route will be open with effect from to-morrow?'

'It will—unless you hear to the contrary from me or

Algy.'

'Good.' The Air Commodore hurried away.

Biggles turned back to Algy and the sergeant. 'Now this is what I want you to do, Algy. You keep in touch with Sergeant Mansur. If anyone comes asking for Lal Din the sergeant will let you know. You will go to the gate and see the man. Tell him that Lal Din is sick. Don't let him suspect the truth. When the man goes off to report to his boss, as it seems pretty certain that he will, you'll follow him and watch where he goes. Make a note of the place and return here. I shall have to go to Jangpur, but I'll get back as quickly as I can. It may be late to-night or early to-morrow morning. If the route is to open to-morrow I've got to pick up the man who is putting the dope in the machines.'

'Why not tell the fellows up there straight out not to touch any confectionery they find in their machines?'

'Because in five minutes everyone of the station would know what was in the wind—including the spy. He'd escape, and warn his boss in Calcutta. No, I've got to catch him. We're not ready yet to broadcast the story. I'd better warn Frayle that I'm coming.'

Algy's eyes went round when he heard Biggles, on the telephone, tell Squadron Leader Frayle that he was coming right away to take another load of medical supplies to Chungking. Biggles continued: 'I want you to start loading the machine at once—yes, in the ordinary way. I don't mind who knows about it. I shall take off as soon as it's ready. By the way, I may be staying at Jangpur for a day or two, so you might fix me up with a room and a bed.'

To this Frayle apparently agreed, for as Biggles hung up he said with a smile, 'That's okay.'

Said Algy: 'Are you really going to Chungking?'

'No fear. I've too much to do here. But I'd like the

gent at Jangpur who hands out the dope to *think* I'm going.'

'Ah,' breathed Algy. 'I get it.'

'I'll be getting along,' decided Biggles. 'You watch things at this end. I hope I shan't be long away.'

In a few minutes, having ascertained that the radiator had been repaired, Biggles was in the air, in the Typhoon heading north on the short run to Jangpur. A haversack containing his small-kit went with him.

Squadron Leader Frayle and Flying Officer Bargent met him on the tarmac, Frayle to say that the transport plane was ready, and Bargent to ask if he could go as second pilot. Biggles refused, gently, but firmly. 'I have reasons of my own for making this trip alone,' he said. 'With luck you should be able to take a machine through yourself, to-morrow.' Turning to Frayle, Biggles asked, 'Did you fix me up with a room?' On receiving an assurance that the room was available he walked over to look at it, and leave his haversack.

Bargent had wandered off, so Biggles was able to speak privately to the station commander who, without asking questions, nevertheless made it clear that there was something about this projected trip that struck him as phoney.

Biggles decided to take him into his confidence. 'The facts, briefly, are these, Frayle,' he said quietly. 'This route has got to start functioning again to-morrow. There's nothing phoney about that. More pilots and machines are being sent up to you. Unfortunately you've got an enemy agent on the station. You can't operate while he's about, so I'm here to nab him. If I succeed, you should have no further trouble. That machine standing out there ticking over has been tampered with—or at least, I hope it has. I've given the saboteur plenty of time to do his dirty work. Now then:

after I have taken off certain things will happen that may surprise you. My subsequent behaviour, for example. But whatever happens I want you to carry on as though everything was normal. And see that your officers do, too. Don't let there be any discussion. Show no surprise, and leave me alone. That's all. I'll push along now.'

'It's your funeral,' murmured Frayle simply. He was too good an officer to argue.

Leaving his small-kit in his room, in mellow evening sunlight Biggles walked across to where the Wellington was waiting. There were several airmen and native porters standing about, watching with interest, but they said nothing. Appearing not to notice them Biggles climbed into his seat, tested his engines, waved the attendant mechanics away, and took off.

As soon as his wheels were off the ground he put the aircraft on a course that was practically due east, for Chungking, and when he settled down he examined the contents of the locker. Conveniently placed, he found a packet of chewing-gum. Smiling grimly he put it in his pocket.

The aircraft roared on through the fading light. The time, by the watch in front of him, was a quarter to six.

Chapter 14
The Trap

Precisely half an hour later, in the silvery light of a full moon, Biggles roared back to the airfield at Jangpur and landed. The return of the aircraft caused minor sensation. Mechanics appeared, running, and there was some brisk conversation when the transport machine was identified. The few remaining officers on the station, mostly ground staff, but with Frayle and Bargent among them, came out to see what was going on. In the clear moonlight this did not take them long.

Biggles climbed out. He seemed to be not quite steady on his feet, and after swaying for a moment rested a hand on an airman's shoulder as if for support.

'What's the matter?' asked Frayle anxiously. 'Why did you come back?'

'Engine—giving trouble,' answered Biggles in a dull voice. 'Getting a—lot of—vibration—starboard side. Thought I'd better—turn back . . . not risk—forced landing.'

'I should think so,' agreed Frayle, looking at Biggles with a curious expression on his face. 'Are you feeling all right—yourself, I mean?'

'No. Feel sort of—odd,' replied Biggles, holding his head in a dazed sort of way. 'Must have got—touch of sun. Twinge of fever—maybe.' He staggered and nearly fell.

The audience of airmen and porters whispered among themselves. There was a titter of laughter when a voice was heard to say, 'Tight as an owl.'

'I think you'd better go to your room and lie down,' suggested Frayle.

'Yes,' muttered Biggles thickly. 'Best thing—I think. Head's sort of—swimming. Must be—fever. Seems to be getting—worse.'

Frayle made a signal and the ambulance came out to meet the party. Biggles allowed the station commander to help him into it.

'Shall I send the M.O. along to see you?' offered Frayle.

'No, thanks. I'll be—all right. Go—sleep.'

'As you like,' returned Frayle.

The ambulance took Biggles to the sleeping accommodation that had been prepared for him—a small room in the station commander's bungalow, which was an extension of the officers' quarters. Most of the officers went back to the mess, but Frayle and Bargent, having removed Biggles' tunic, helped him on to the bed and took off his shoes. He appeared to fall asleep immediately.

Said Bargent, looking down at the recumbent figure: 'I've got a nasty feeling there's something fishy about this. If I hadn't done a trip with him I'd swear he was three sheets in the wind.'

'He half prepared me for something unusual,' replied Frayle. 'He said that whatever happened I was not to worry him, but leave him alone. I don't like leaving a fellow in this condition, but I suppose we shall have to.' They went out, leaving the electric light on.

As soon as they had gone Biggles raised himself on an elbow, listened intently for a minute, and then got off the bed. Moving quickly he switched out the light, locked the door, drew the curtains aside and arranged the window so that it could be opened easily. For a little while he stood surveying the airfield, a clear view of which the window commanded, while pale blue moonlight flooded the little room. Leaving the window he took out his automatic, examined it, and put it in a side pocket of the slacks he still wore. The time, he noted, was twenty minutes to seven. Then, apparently satisfied, he settled himself on the bed in a sleeping position facing the window, and half closed his eyes.

Time passed. For a while there were occasional sounds outside—footsteps of airmen going on or off duty, and voices as they talked or called to each other. But as the night wore on these sounds died away and silence fell. After a short interval the orderly officer* could be heard making his first round. More time passed. Once, far away, a dog or a jackal yelped. A cock crowed in a distant village, apparently misled by the brilliant moonlight into thinking that dawn was at hand. Biggles did not move a muscle. Only his chest rose and fell with his deep breathing. The difficulty, he found, was to do this without actually falling asleep, for he was beginning to feel the strain of working at high pressure, and he was really tired. His eyes, half closed, were on the window. Not for a moment did they leave it.

He lost count of time, but he estimated roughly that it was about nine-thirty when he saw that for which he had so long waited. There was no sound, but a shadow moved slowly across the square of moonlight framed by the window. Within a minute it was back, stationary, close by the window. All this Biggles saw quite clearly through half-closed eyes. Moonlight flashed on the glass of the window as inch by inch it was opened. Still there was no noise, and as the man crept into the room Biggles marvelled that anyone could move with

* The officer on duty for the day

149

such a complete absence of sound. Standing close against the window, the visitor made no more noise than the vague shadow he appeared to be. Biggles could not make out any detail. Beyond the fact that the visitor was naked except for a loin-cloth, and carrying in his left hand a strip of rag, he could see nothing of him.

Like a black wraith the marauder appeared to float towards the bed. Again he stopped and listened, before bending over the prone form on the bed as if to examine it. His breathing was just audible. Then, taking the strip of rag in both hands he pressed it firmly over Biggles' lips and nostrils.

As the rag touched his face Biggles' hands shot up and seized his assailant by the throat. With a convulsive jerk the man broke free, and Biggles knew that he had made a mistake; for the throat was slimy with oil, and his fingers could not maintain their grip. The man streaked like a panther to the window. Launching himself from the bed Biggles got him by the legs: but they, too, had been oiled, and although the man fell, he was free again before Biggles could take advantage of the fall. The body slid through his hands like an eel. In a flash the man was on his feet. Biggles, too, was getting up. He caught the gleam of steel and flung himself sideways, but a sharp pain in the upper part of his left arm told him that the knife had found a billet. After the first stab there was no more pain; only a feeling of nausea.

By this time his assailant had turned, and had again reached the window. Biggles, by this time aware of the futility of trying to hold the body, grabbed at the loin-cloth, and tried to drag the man back into the room. But either the stuff was rotten, or in two pieces, for the part he had seized came away in his hand, with the result that he went over backwards. By the time he had recovered himself, although he was still on the floor, the man was half-way across the sill, a black silhouette against the moonlight. It was obvious that in another second he would be gone.

Now Biggles' plan had been to catch the man alive, for which reason he had so far refrained from using his pistol; but seeing that the man was about to escape, and aware that if he succeeded in this it would be fatal to his plans, he snatched out his pistol. There was no time to take aim. He fired from the hip. The weapon roared. The flash momentarily blinded him, so that he could not see whether he had hit his man or into. Vaguely conscious of hot blood running down his arm he scrambled to his feet and dashed to the window. One glance told him all he needed to know. A figure lay asprawl on the brown earth. Panting, for the last few minutes had been strenuous, Biggles backed to the bed and sat down heavily, to recover his breath and his composure.

Outside, voices shouted. Footsteps approached, running, both inside and outside the bungalow. A fist banged on the door. Before Biggles could answer, or get to it, it was forced open with a crash. Someone blundered into the room. The light was switched on. Frayle, in pyjamas, stood there.

'What happened?' he asked sharply. 'Who fired that shot?'

'I did,' replied Biggles laconically.

'Good God, man! You're wounded.' Frayle's eyes were on the bloodstained sleeve of Biggles' shirt.

'It's only a scratch,' returned Biggles. 'Give me a drink—water will do.'

Frayle obliged.

'Thanks.' Biggles drank, and drew a deep breath.

151

'That's better. Send for the M.O., Frayle, to have a look at that fellow outside. Tell him to bring his needle and cotton—my arm may need a stitch.'

Bargent entered through the window. 'I say!' he exclaimed, in a perturbed voice, 'You've killed the fellow.'

'I'm sorry about that—in a way,' replied Biggles. 'I wanted him alive. Who is he—do you know?'

'Of course I know. It's Kong Po, our *dhobi-wallah**.'

'What was his nationality?'

'We always supposed he was a sort of Chinese.'

Frayle spoke: 'He's Chinese according to his station identity card.'

'Alter it to Japanese,' cried Biggles.

Presently the M.O. came in. 'There's nothing I can do for that fellow outside—he's dead,' he announced. 'What about your arm?' He looked at the wound. 'Narrow, but rather deep,' he went on. 'You'd better have a stitch in it.'

'Go ahead,' invited Biggles. 'Don't be long; I've got to get back to Dum Dum. Give me a cigarette, Frayle.'

'Before you go, perhaps you won't mind telling me why you came here to bump off my *dhobi?*' Frayle's voice was soft with sarcasm.

'I didn't come here to shoot him,' replied Biggles evenly. 'I came here to get him, but he knifed me and I daren't let him get away. Too much was at stake.'

'Why did you want him?'

'Because,' answered Biggles, flinching as the M.O.'s needle pricked his skin, 'he was your own pet secret weapon. He came to this room to strangle me. I thought he would come. I hoped he would. One of our airmen

---

* Indian military term for laundryman. From Hindustani *dhob* = washing.

at Dum Dum, a sergeant named Gray, was murdered in precisely the same circumstances and for the same reason. I planned for a repetition of the incident, and it came off. Your precious Kong Po was afraid I might put two and two together, and talk about it, when I came round from what he supposed was a stupor brought on by a drug.'

'But I don't understand,' said Frayle impatiently. 'How does this hook up with the secret weapon?'

'I'll tell you in plain language,' decided Biggles. 'Keep the story to yourself though, for the time being. There isn't a secret weapon—or not the sort you probably have in mind. The enemy has planted agents on certain of our airfields. With so many Orientals about that wasn't difficult. The master-brain behind the racket had enough influence to get these men jobs. In our case, at Dum Dum, the spy was a mess waiter. The real work of these men was simple. All they had to do was arrange for a small supply of chocolate or chewing-gum to be put in each operational aircraft just before it took off. These sweeties were not the sort you'd give to the baby to suck. They had been treated with a powerful narcotic. It needs little imagination to visualise what happened in the aircraft. During the course of the flight the pilot finds the confectionery and has a bite, with the result that he loses the use of his limbs and his brain and crashes. It was always on the boards, however, that the stuff might fall into the hands of someone other than the man for whom it was intended. The sergeant I mentioned just now got hold of a piece. During the night, while he was still under the influence of the drug, he was murdered to prevent him from talking. I didn't know how it was done, but I do now. Strangulation was the method employed; I imagine it isn't hard to strangle an unconscious man without leaving a mark. This evening I set a trap. I took off but returned, ostensibly with engine trouble. There was dope in the machine. When I landed I acted as though I had fallen for it. Some of your fellows thought I was drunk. Only the spy, who was pretty certain to investigate, would know the truth—or what he thought was the truth. That I had been drugged. It was up to him to see that I didn't come round, so he came to do me in. I was waiting, with the result that he got it, not me. That's all. Now he's out of the way there won't be any more doped confectionery in your machines, so with effect from to-morrow the route will operate in the normal way. But to be on the safe side— you needn't say why—you can issue a secret order to your pilots forbidding them to touch any sort of food while in the air. In any case, I'm aiming to clean up the whole gang in the next few hours. Meanwhile, for obvious reasons, you will say nothing of this to anyone. Should someone come here inquiring for Kong Po— and that may happen—just say that he has met with an accident and is not available.'

'Well, stiffen my benders!' muttered Bargent. 'I never heard such a tale in my life.'

'The East is the home of strange stories.' returned Biggles dryly, as he tried moving his arm, which the M.O. had now finished bandaging.

'What beats me is, how you got on the trail of the thing,' said Frayle, in a voice of wonder. 'It was so simple, yet so subtle—'

'The Oriental mind works on those lines. I've been in the East before,' murmured Biggles as he stood up. 'I'll just have a look round this *dhobi-wallah's* bedroom and then get back to Dum Dum.'

As Frayle led the way to the room Biggles asked: 'How did you come to employ this man—Kong Po?'

'A fellow in Calcutta rang me up and asked me if I had a vacancy for a good man. He said Kong Po had worked for him, so he could recommend him. The chap was out of work and he wanted to help him. So I took Kong Po on.'

'You knew this man who rang you up, I presume? I mean, he wasn't just a stranger?'

'Oh, no. I've met him several times. As a matter of fact he's a wealthy merchant who has often made presents to the mess. I wish there were more about like him.'

A ghost of a smile hovered for a moment round Biggles' lips. 'Was his name by any chance Larapindi?'

Frayle started. 'Yes. What on earth made you say that?'

'Only that he has showed an interest in Dum Dum, too,' replied Biggles casually.

The room turned out to be a tiny cubicle near the kitchens. A systematic search revealed only one item of interest—a small cardboard box containing several loose bars of chocolate, wrapped, and packets of chewing-gum. The box bore in large type the usual confectionery manufacturer's announcements, under the heading: CHARNEYS GOLD MEDAL CHOCOLATES. LONDON. AGENCIES AT CALCUTTA, CAPE TOWN, SINGAPORE AND SYDNEY,

'Very interesting,' murmured Biggles. 'As the stuff is loose we may assume that the box is merely a receptacle for the present contents which, I imagine, have been doctored. I doubt if the man had any hand in the preparation of the dope; the chocolate and gum would be issued to him in this form, ready for use. Better burn the stuff, Frayle, to prevent accidents.'

A corporal medical orderly came in. In his hand he carried a packet of notes, brand new. 'I thought you'd better take charge of this, sir,' he said, speaking to his station commander. 'I found it tied up in Kong Po's loin-cloth. There must be close on a thousand rupees— a lot of money for a man like that to have about him.'

'Too much for an honest *dhobi-wallah*,' said Biggles softly. 'I'll take charge of that, Frayle, if you don't mind; I have an idea it will tell us something. Well, there doesn't seem to be anything else; I think I'll be getting along.'

'Sure you feel fit enough to fly?' queried the M.O.

'I'm all right, thanks,' answered Biggles. 'Arm's getting a bit stiff, that's all—but I don't fly with my left hand.'

In twenty minutes he was back at Dum Dum. The time was just after ten o'clock. He went straight to Air Commodore Raymond's quarter. The Air Commodore was there, writing a report.

'I thought it would ease your mind to know that the Chungking run is okay now, sir.' reported Biggles. 'The regular service will be resumed in the morning. Things are moving fast, and may move faster before dawn. While I'm talking to my chaps I want you to do something for me.'

'Certainly.'

Biggles took from his pocket the notes that had been found on the dead *dhobi-wallah*. 'From the condition these are in it seems likely that they were issued recently,' he surmised. 'I want you to find out which bank issued these notes, and to whom.'

The Air Commodore looked dubious. 'At this hour? People will have knocked off work.'

'Then tell them to knock on again,' requested Biggles. 'This business won't wait. You ought to be able to get the information on the 'phone.'

'I'll try,' promised the Air Commodore. 'I take it

you've got the enemy agent at Jangpur ear-marked?'

Biggles was at the door. He looked over his shoulder, smiling grimly. 'I ear-marked him all right—with a forty-five pistol slug. See you later.'

He went on to the mess. Algy and the rest were there, waiting. Some were dozing, but there was a quick, expectant stir, when Biggles entered. He spoke to Bertie.

'Get some coffee and see that it's strong. I'm dog tired, but we're going to be busy for a bit. You might scrounge some sandwiches or biscuits at the same time.' He turned to Algy. 'Did you have any luck?'

'It worked out as you expected,' replied Algy. 'A man calling himself Lal Din's brother rolled up, asking for him. I told him Lal Din was sick. He went off and I followed him.'

'Good. Where did he go?'

'To the docks, to the warehouse of Tahil and Larap-indi. I hung around for some time but he didn't come out, although there seemed to be a fair amount of activity.'

'There'll be more, presently,' promised Biggles. 'I fancy that warehouse is the target for to-night. I'm just waiting for confirmation. I shall be glad when this show is over; I'm missing my beauty sleep. Ah—here's the coffee.'

'What happened at Jangpur?' asked Ginger. 'The others have told me what happened here.'

Biggles gave a brief account of events at Jangpur. He had just finished when the Air Commodore came in.

'I got the information you wanted,' he announced. 'I'm afraid you'll be disappointed; the money seems to have been issued in the ordinary course of business.'

'It would be,' mutter Biggles cynically.

'It's part of a pay-roll issued by the Peninsular and Oriental Bank, to—just a minute.' The Air Commodore fumbled with a slip of paper.

'Tahil and Larapindi?' suggested Biggles.

The Air Commodore stared. 'That's right. How the deuce did you guess that?'

'I wasn't guessing,' returned Biggles. 'Thanks, sir. You can go to bed now. I may have some good news for you in the morning.'

'Are you going out?'

'We are.'

'Can I come?'

Biggles shook his head. 'You'd be better advised to keep out of the way. What 666 Squadron is going to do, or may have to do, to-night, is entirely unofficial. There's no place for an Air Commodore.'

'All right. I'll leave you to it.' The Air Commodore looked at Biggles suspiciously. 'Be careful.' He went out.

'Are we really going down to this warehouse place?' asked Tug.

'Probably. It depends. I have a call to make first.'

'But I say, old boy, it's a bit late for making calls, isn't it?' queried Bertie.

'Not too late, I hope.'

'Say! Suppose there's nobody at the warehouse?' put in Tex. 'How shall we get in?'

'It was never my intention to ring the front-door bell,' said Biggles. His manner became brisk. 'Algy, see about transport. Better get a light truck, one we can all get in. And in case there's an argument you'd better all bring guns. On the other hand, there may be nothing for you to do. We shall see. Ginger, you're about the best fitter in the party. Put a few tools in a bag in case we have to do a spot of housebreaking.

Which reminds me; I think it would be a good idea if everyone wore tennis shoes, or something with a sole that won't make a noise.'

'Where do we go first?' asked Algy.

Biggles went to the telephone directory, looked up a number and made a note. 'I want you to drive me first to Mimosa Lodge, Razlet Avenue. If I remember, that's one of those wide streets in the European quarter east of the Maidan. I'll guide you.'

'What are you going to do there?' asked Algy.

'I'm only going to make a call.'

'On whom?'

'A gentleman by the name of Larapindi,' answered Biggles.

Chapter 15
Biggles Makes A Call

Algy drove the car, a light, covered service lorry, to Calcutta. Biggles sat on one side of him, with Ginger on his left.

On the short drive in Biggles said: 'I can't tell you exactly what I'm going to do because I'm not sure myself. The business has reached that touchy stage when anything can happen. I'm a bit scared of the plan I have in mind, but our hands are being forced. We've got to move fast, before the enemy learns what has happened to his operatives at Dum Dum and Jangpur. I'm pretty sure this fellow Larapindi is in the racket, and if he's not actually the head man, he's pretty high up. The broad idea, if I find Larapindi at home, is: first, to allay his suspicions, if they are aroused; and secondly, to get him to do something that will give us the necessary evidence to hang him.'

'Couldn't we get the police to raid his premises, both his home and the warehouse?' suggested Algy.

'We could, and that is what the police would probably do if they knew what we know. But I don't think it would do the slightest good. It's ten to one they wouldn't find anything. Spies aren't such fools as to leave incriminating evidence lying about when they know the police are on the job. Police actions are governed by regulations. They have to announce their intentions by knocking at the door. If we asked for a police raid the chances are we should do more harm than good, by exposing our hand for nothing. I've always

160

taken the view that when one is dealing with tricksters the best plan is to play tricky. So I'm going to try unorthodox tactics. If I slip up there will be an awful stink—a question asked in Parliament, perhaps. We shall get a rap over the knuckles, and perhaps lose some seniority.'

'That should worry us,' remarked Algy sarcastically.

'We'll stop the car a little distance from the house,' went on Biggles. 'Here's the Maidan. I believe that's the Avenue Razlet, over there. Pull up against the kerb when I give the word.'

In view of the lateness of the hour—it was nearly eleven o'clock—there were few pedestrians about, and very little traffic. The night was fine and hot. The Hugli River wound like a monstrous black snake through the resting city.

'You'll do,' said Biggles sharply. As the car pulled up he continues: 'Tell the boys to keep quiet while I'm away. If I'm not back in an hour you'll know something's gone wrong, so you'd better come looking for me. If you do, remember that unless my suspicions are all cock-eye, this Larapindi is as cunning as a jackal and as deadly as a cobra. Sit fast and keep your eyes on the house. I may be some time.'

Biggles walked on up the avenue. A policeman directed him to Mimosa Lodge, a magnificent house standing in its own spacious garden. A fine pair of wrought iron gates gave access to a short drive that ended at a sweeping flight of steps. The gates were not locked, and in a minute Biggles was pressing the bell.

The door was opened, as he expected it to be, by a servant, quiet, efficient, in spotless white. The man looked a trifle surprised when he saw the visitor, but in reply to Biggles' inquiry said that Mr. Larapindi was at home. Biggles presented his card, and was then asked to wait in a hall, the furnishings of which were so fine, so rare and so costly as to give him a twinge of uneasiness. The house appeared to be the residence of a millionaire rather than that of an enemy spy. While the servant had gone to deliver his card his eyes roamed from one object of Oriental art to another, with rising misgivings. Then he realised that as a partner in the great firm of Tahil and Larapindi, the man whom he had come to see probably was a millionaire several times over.

The servant, walking with soft, easy steps, returned. 'This way, sahib,' said he.

Biggles followed him through a sumptuously furnished library to a door at the far end. On this the servant knocked before opening it. 'Enter, sahib,' he invited, with a little bow. 'Mr Larapindi awaits you.'

As Biggles accepted the invitation he took in the scene at a glance. The room, not a large one, was fitted out in a manner that was something between a private sitting-room and a study. Again the furnishings were impressive. Pieces of priceless Oriental porcelain, objects in carved ivory and exquisite work in precious metals, occupied the shelves. Behind a large lacquer writing-desk the owner was standing to greet his visitor. He was a small man immaculately dressed in European clothes. Large gold-rimmed spectacles, slightly tinted, almost concealed his eyes.

'Please to be seated, sir,' said Larapindi, in faultless if rather suave English, at the same time indicating a heavily-carved chair that had already been pulled towards the desk in readiness. Having seen his visitor seated he himself sat down behind the desk.

'Thank you,' said Biggles.

'You wish to see me?' went on Larapindi smoothly. 'I do not think we have met before?'

Biggles smiled awkwardly. 'No. This is hardly the time to call, I'm afraid, but when I have explained the reason I hope you'll forgive me. It happened that in passing your house I remembered, or it may have been that your house reminded me, of something my canteen manager once told me. But before I go any further I should explain that I am the temporary Mess President at Dum Dum airfield. Some time ago, Sergeant Mansur, our canteen manager, informed me that you have been good enough to recommend a man for work in the canteen. His name is Lal Din—or perhaps you don't remember him?'

'I recall him perfectly well,' said Larapindi, in an expressionless voice. He pushed towards Biggles a massive gold cigarette box. 'Please to have a cigarette, sir.'

'Thank you.' Biggles accepted the cigarette. 'This man Lal Din has turned out to be a most excellent steward—always cheerful, willing and obliging. We shall miss him.'

Larapindi's chin dropped a trifle so that he could survey his guest over his large glasses. 'Do you mean, he has—gone?'

'Not exactly,' returned Biggles. 'But the day before yesterday he complained of not feeling well. Yesterday he was obviously very ill, so I sent the Medical Officer to see him. It turns out that the poor fellow has smallpox.'

Larapindi drew a deep breath. 'Oh, dear! That is very sad.'

Biggles thought he caught a suspicion of relief, or it may have been understanding, in the way the words were spoken.

'Of course, it hardly needs me to tell you what an outbreak of infectious disease means on a station like

Dum Dum,' he went on. 'Lal Din, poor chap, has been put in an isolation ward, and there, I'm afraid, he'll remain for some time. Which brings me to my point. We're going to miss him. To-morrow morning I shall have to see about getting a new steward. In the ordinary way I should have advertised for a man, but this evening I had to come into the city, and in passing your house it struck me suddenly that as your first recommendation had turned out so successfully you might know of another fellow. I don't expect you to produce another Lal Din off-hand, so to speak; but you might know of someone who could take up his duties right away. We shall be short-handed without Lal Din, and the sooner I have someone to replace him the better. In the ordinary way that might take two or three days. Now you know the reason I hope you will pardon me for breaking in on you at so late an hour.'

Larapindi made a deprecatory gesture. 'Do not speak of it,' he protested. 'Call on me at any time. If I can be of service the honour will be mine. It happens that you have called at a most fortunate moment. Only to-day my business manager came to me telling me of a man who has applied to us for work, a most excellent man. I should be glad to employ him myself, but I shall account it an honour if you will allow me to send him to you. I forget his name for the moment, but he is a Burmese from Rangoon, one of those unfortunate creatures who had to fly to India before the invasion of these hateful Japanese. He has been a house servant, and has had experience as a waiter. When would you like me to send him to you?'

'First thing in the morning,' requested Biggles. 'The sooner he takes up his duties the sooner will the pressure on our overworked staff be relieved.'

'I shall see that he is there,' promised Larapindi.

'Thank you. That is really most kind of you,' said Biggles gratefully. 'By the way, on my last tour of duty in India I believe I once had the pleasure of meeting Mr. Tahil, the senior partner of your firm. I trust he is in good health?'

'Alas, no,' sighed Larapindi sadly. 'Evidently you did not hear of his tragic accident?'

'Why, what happened?' asked Biggles, who was genuinely surprised, and not a little interested.

'Poor Mr. Tahil died from snake-bite,' explained Larapindi. 'It happened on a golf links, of all places. His ball fell in the rough. Stooping to pick it up he accidentally touched a *krait** that must have been lying beside the ball. Unfortunately, we were some way from the club-house. I ran all the way, but it was no use. Before a doctor could arrive with serum he was dead. It was a lamentable affair, and caused something of a sensation in Calcutta, because Mr Tahil was a noted philanthropist, besides being a good servant of the government.'

Biggles' eyes were on Larapindi's face. 'What a terrible shock it must have been to you. I take it you were playing together?'

'We were. It was indeed a shock. I've hardly recovered from it.'

'And a blow, too, I imagine,' murmured Biggles sympathetically. 'I mean, his death must have thrown a lot of extra work on your shoulders, since it would leave you in complete charge of the business.'

Larapindi shrugged. 'These things happen; we must face them. I am doing my best to carry on single-handed.'

---

* A small but extremely poisonous Indian snake. Its bite is usually fatal in a few minutes.

Biggles shook his head. 'I am very sorry to learn of this.'

Now, during the latter part of the conversation his eyes lifted to a framed photograph that hung on the wall behind his host. Actually, there were several such photographs, most of them portraying the various offices of the firm of Tahil and Larapindi throughout the Orient. But one photograph in particular claimed his attention, for it was a picture of an aircraft, a civil marine aircraft—or to be more precise, a Gull. It was moored on a river, off the end of the slipway, with a private hangar bearing the name of the firm in the background. The aircraft, which carried the Indian registration letters VTT-XQL, also bore on its nose the name of the firm.

'Pardon my curiosity, Mr. Larapindi,' said Biggles, 'but the photograph behind you arouses my professional interest. I see your firm operates its own aircraft?'

'It did, until the war put an end to private enterprise,' answered Larapindi, swinging round in his chair to glance at the photograph. 'We try to be progressive, you know. Our interests in the East are so widespread that the adoption of the aeroplane as a means of transport was almost automatic. We bought a machine, a Gull, and established a repair and maintenance depot a few miles higher up the river. It would have been developed had not the war put an end to our plans—only temporarily, I hope.'

'Of course,' said Biggles quietly. 'No doubt you had to ground the machine when the war started.'

'Yes, the government asked us to, and, naturally, we were only too anxious to oblige. We shall need pilots when the war is over, so if ever you abandon the service as a career I hope you will come to see me, to our mutual benefit.'

'I'll bear it in mind,' promised Biggles. 'But I must be on my way. I'm glad to have had this opportunity of meeting you.' He got up.

'I hope we shall meet again, sir,' said Larapindi, also rising.

'I'm sure we shall,' replied Biggles evenly. 'Meanwhile, I shall expect your man first thing in the morning.'

'He will be there.'

Larapindi saw his guest to the door, where they parted.

Biggles returned to the lorry.

'How did you get on?' asked Algy.

'I got what I went for,' answered Biggles. 'Now listen, everybody. I've told Larapindi that Lal Din is down with smallpox, and asked him to send us a man to replace him. He has promised to send one along first thing in the morning. That means he's got to get busy, to-night, finding a man, giving him instructions, and supplying him with a stock of doped confectionery. I doubt if he'll risk talking over the telephone. Unless I've missed my mark he'll attend to the business in person. We'll watch from here. If he goes out, we'll follow.'

Hardly had he finished speaking when a man, in the attire of an Indian servant, appeared at the iron gates, and walked briskly down the avenue.

'What about him?' asked Ginger.

'He's probably part of the organisation, but we've got to go for bigger game,' answered Biggles. 'That chap has been sent out on an errand—probably to fetch the fellow Larapindi has in mind to replace Lal Din. We're all right. Either the man will be brought here, in which case we shall know it, or he will be taken

167

somewhere else. If he is taken somewhere else, Larapindi will have to go out to see him. Ah! What's this?'

A servant had appeared at the gates and opened them wide. A minute later an expensive touring car crept through. The gates were closed. The car cruised away down the avenue.

'After him,' ordered Biggles crisply. 'Keep the car in sight, but don't get too close.'

'What about the Tahil part of the partnership?' asked Algy, as they followed the car. 'Aren't you interested in him?'

'Tahil is dead,' answered Biggles slowly. 'He was bitten by a snake while playing golf with Larapindi. Since it must have suited Larapindi remarkably well to be left alone in charge of the business, I have a feeling that there were two snakes on the links that morning. But let's discuss that presently.'

Five minutes later it was clear that the car was heading for the dock area.

'It looks as if he's going to the warehouse,' said Algy. 'This is the direction, anyway.'

This surmise turned out to be correct. The car stopped before the main entrance of the establishment of Tahil and Larapindi. The lorry had also stopped, some distance away, but close enough for Biggles to see Larapindi alight and enter the building. The car was driven back a little way, revealing that it had a chauffeur in charge, to be parked in a narrow turning, one side of which was entirely occupied by the warehouse.

'It looks as though he's going to be some time, otherwise the car would have waited at the front entrance,' remarked Biggles. 'It's a bigger building than I expected,' he added, taking stock of the warehouse and its position. Not that much could be seen. The building, a vast square pile, stood alone, separated from similar warehouses which lined that side of the road by narrow streets. It fronted the main road. The rear part, which seemed to be much older than the front, which was obviously modern, overlooked the broad, turgid, Hugli River.

'When I saw it in daylight, the place gave me the impression of being a very old building with a new front stuck on it,' said Algy. 'It's pretty ramshackle at the back.'

'Most warehouses are, or those I've seen,' answered Biggles. 'Hello, here's another car stopping. It's a taxi.'

The taxi pulled up at the front entrance, deposited two passengers and drove on.

'We're doing fine,' murmured Biggles. 'One of those fellows is Larapindi's servant, the one we saw leave the house. The other must be the man he went to fetch— the man Larapindi is going to send along to replace Lal Din. Brought him in a taxi eh? Must be in a hurry. This is how I hoped it would pan out. If I'm right, Larapindi is going to give that fellow his instructions. Instructions wouldn't be much use without the dope, so it must be kept here. This is where we take a hand. Listen everybody. Algy and Ginger will come with me. We've got to get into that building somehow. Bertie, you'll take charge of the rest of the party. Leave some-one here to look after the lorry. Post the others round the building to see that no one gets out. If you hear shots, or anything that sounds like a row, break in and lend a hand.'

'Why not wait for this new assistant to come out and grab him with the goods on him?' suggested Johnny Crisp.

'I'm not interested in him,' answered Biggles. 'The man I want is Larapindi, and we've got to catch him handling the dope, or he'll slip through our fingers like a wet fish. Come on, Algy. Come on, Ginger—bring your bag.'

In a minute they were on the pavement, at a corner of the big warehouse. Biggles set off down a side turning, looking at the windows. 'We've got to get in without making a noise,' he said quietly. He continued walking until they had nearly reached the river, and then pulled up by a door, a side entrance to the building. As a matter of course he turned the handle, to find, as he expected, that the door was locked. He turned to Ginger. 'What have you got in that bag?'

'I've got a hacksaw, a file, some tyre levers; a drill—'

'Good. The drill ought to do the trick,' interrupted Biggles. 'Make a hole near the handle, and cut out a piece of wood big enough to get a hand through. The key will probably be in the lock on the inside.'

This conjecture proved to be correct; but ten minutes were occupied in cutting the hole. Ginger did the work while Biggles and Algy kept watch. As it happened no one passed through the little street, so the work was not interrupted. As soon as the hole had been made Biggles inserted a hand, and with an exclamation of satisfaction brought out the key. He inserted it in the lock on the outside. As the door swung open, the warm, aromatic aroma of mixed Indian merchandise, tea, spices, jute, oilseeds and grain, poured out to greet them. Without a sound they stepped inside. Biggles closed the door. There was a faint snick as he switched on his torch. Its beam stabbed the darkness.

Chapter 16
The Green Idol

Not until he was inside the building did Biggles realise fully the size of it, and the problem this presented. It was apparent, however, that they were in that part devoted to the storage of merchandise, and by the character of it, the export department. Cases of tea, sacks of grain, bales and boxes stood stacked in orderly array from floor to ceiling, with narrow corridors between to permit the passage of those whose business it was to handle these goods. To Biggles, it seemed unlikely that Larapindi would conduct his affairs in that section of the building; it was almost certain that he would be somewhere in the administrative department, and with the object of finding this he set off, moving quietly but quickly along a corridor that ran parallel with the narrow street outside, in the direction of the front entrance. Algy and Ginger followed close behind. The reek of the goods was not unpleasant, but it was almost overpowering in its pungency.

After a little while, however, this smell began perceptibly to change, and the reason was soon evident. There was a break in the ranks of merchandise, and on the far side of the passage thus made the type of produce changed abruptly. Here, now, were wood and cardboard boxes bearing the names of British and United States manufacturers; clearly, the import department. Once Biggles stopped, and without speaking pointed to a large notice stencilled on one of the cases. The words were CHARNEYS, LONDON. CONFECTIONERY.

Biggles continued to walk forward, and presently perceived that he was nearing his first objective — the administrative block. The merchandise ended, to give way to numerous passages, with wood-partitioned offices, some large, some small, bearing the names of wholesale and retail departments and the names of their managers. Biggles' progress became slower and more cautious.

So far not a sound of any sort had broken the tomb-like silence of the warehouse; but now, passing an unpretentious staircase there came from somewhere in the distance, high above, no louder than the rustle of dry leaves, a murmur of voices. Biggles hesitated for a moment and then went on. He did not go far, being brought to a halt when the passage ended at swing doors, panelled with panes of frosted glass, through which came a feeble but steady light. Switching out his torch, and laying a finger on his lips for silence, he made a stealthy reconnaissance. Then, with infinite care, he allowed the door to sink back into place and turned to the others.

'It's the main hall,' he breathed. 'There's a man on duty inside the front door. We can't go any farther this way without being seen. We shall have to go back.' He retreated as far as the narrow stairway, and after listening for a little while to the distant sound of talking began a discreet ascent.

The staircase, after making two right-angle turns, ended in a corridor on the first floor, lighted by a single electric bulb. The corridor extended for some distance on either side, with doors at frequent intervals. All were shut. It was now possible to distinguish a single voice, a voice of authority it seemed, speaking rapidly. It still came from above. Biggles explored, and half a dozen paces along the corridor found another staircase leading upwards. It was precisely the same as the first, and for practical purposes a continuation of it. It mounted to the second floor, to another corridor identical with that of the floor below. The voice still came from above. Another advance took Biggles and his companions to the third floor. Still the voice came from higher up. It was now fairly clear, but after listening for a moment Biggles shrugged his shoulders. He could not identify the language, much less make out what was being said.

Farther upward progress was now barred by a door on which a single word had been painted in white letters in several languages. One of the languages was English. The word was PRIVATE. Biggles tried the door. It opened readily, revealing another staircase. But this one was different. On the floors below the boards had been left bare; here they were covered by a thick red carpet. After a slight inclination of his head Biggles went on up to the next floor, into an atmosphere altogether different from those down below. Gone, now, was any impression of a warehouse or business office. The appointments were those of a luxury hotel, or a suite in a block of expensive flats. The staircase ended in what might best be described as an outer hall of some size, richly furnished and carpeted. Around this hall, opposite the intruders as they stood at the head of the staircase, were four doors. One stood ajar. The room to which it gave entrance was lighted, but it was not from here that the voice came. It was the room next to it.

Biggles looked at the others with a puzzled expression on his face. He did not speak, but by a gesture indicated what he was thinking. Indeed, something was now explained that had puzzled Ginger all the way up the stairs—the loudness of the voice inside the room. It did not speak in an ordinary conversational tone, but was pitched high as though it were reading aloud to an audience. No explanation of this being forthcoming, after a little grimace to indicate his lack of understanding, Biggles crossed the hall to the open door, and without touching it, peeped in. A faint click of the tongue, denoting surprise, brought the others to his side. Very slowly he pushed the door wide open so that the whole interior of the room could be seen. Strictly speaking it was not a room. It was a laboratory.

After a swift survey of the scene Biggles paid no attention to the scientific apparatus that stood about, or the rows of jars and bottles that occupied the numerous shelves. He went straight to a bench on which had been accumulated an assortment of objects, a curious assortment—curious because they were not what one would expect to find in a laboratory. Most conspicuous were two cardboard boxes, bearing in bold type a name, and certain announcements, which to Biggles were becoming familiar. The name was Charneys. Both boxes had been broken open and part of their contents strewn on the bench. In one case it was chewing gum; in the other, chocolate. Near these was a pile of loose wrapping-papers, some pink, some brown, that had obviously been torn carelessly from the products named on the boxes. The contents of the wrapping-papers, however, were not there. Close at hand, in two separate boxes, were identical wrapping-papers, but these were brand new. There were only two other objects on the bench, but they were significant. One was a small glass jar half filled with an oily, colourless liquid, and the other, a case across which lay a hypodermic syringe.

It needed less time to observe these things than to describe them, and after a long penetrating stare

Biggles said softly: 'This is it. We're in the dope shop. Larapindi didn't lose any time preparing samples for the new man to distribute at Dum Dum. This little collection tells the whole story. He take the stuff as it arrives from England, unwraps as much as he needs, gives each sample a shot of dope with the needle, and rewraps it in a new paper. He can't inject much dope into a solid bar of chocolate, but no doubt one drop would be ample to knock out anyone not used to the stuff. I knew a fellow who once chewed a piece of charas—the dope that's most popular in India. To be on the safe side he nibbled a piece only half the size of an orange pip, but he went out as if he'd been hit on the head with a rolling-pin. We may assume that the stuff in that bottle is highly concentrated. I'd like to make Larapindi drink the lot. That's him talking in the next room; I recognise his voice, although what he has to shout about I don't know. We've enough evidence here to hang him, so let's see what he has to say about it. There may be some slight argument when he sees us, so have your guns handy. Algy, you stay here and don't let anybody touch this stuff. I'd like Raymond to see it just as it is. Come on, Ginger,' as he finished speaking Biggles took his automatic from his pocket and slipped into his right sleeve, so that it was held there by his fingers.

Leaving Algy by the bench, followed by Ginger he returned to the hall and walked on to the door through which the voice still came. 'He seems to have a lot to say,' he murmured. 'I shall try to open the door—assuming it isn't locked—without being seen, but I don't think there's much hope of that. I've no idea of how he'll behave when he sees us, but you'd better be ready to move fast. Hold your hat—here we go.'

Biggles' fingers closed firmly over the handle of the

door. Very slowly he turned it. The door moved. A slit of light appeared between door and frame. He released the handle: but instead of the door remaining open only a few inches, as he intended, it continued the opening movement—slowly, but quite definitely.

The result was inevitable. The movement was seen. But before that happened Biggles was granted three seconds' grace to absorb the picture presented to his gaze. It was enough, although what he saw not what he expected. Far from it. He had thought, indeed, he had convinced himself—unwisely, as he later confessed—that there would not be more than three persons in the room; Larapindi, the steward who was to replace Lal Din, and perhaps the servant who had fetched him. Instead, there were not fewer than seven or eight people present. He did not count them. There was no time for that. Not that it mattered much. These men were seated round a large mahogany table, so that the proceedings had the appearance of a board meeting; a strange one, perhaps, because the centre of the table was occupied by a green stone idol. Larapindi was standing at the head of the table, unfortunately for Biggles, at the far end, because in that position he was facing the door. The heads of his disciples, or assistants, or agents, or whatever they were, were bowed in the direction of the idol in reverent adoration.

Now, had this been all, Biggles might have been embarrassed, for he would have been the last man to interrupt a devotional ritual, whatever religion was involved. But it was not all. In front of each man, looking absurdly out of place on account of its blatantly European character, was a little heap of the packets Biggles had come to know so well; packets of chewing-gum and chocolate. This told him all he needed to know. The fact that several agents, instead of one, were being instructed in their duties, and that these agents were obviously being bound to their murderous tasks by a religious ceremony, made no difference to the broad situation. He had, as he had planned, caught the plotters red-handed. That was the dominating factor. Whether he and Ginger would be able to apprehend so many was another matter. They had at least the advantage of surprise.

Larapindi was the first to observe the open door. He must have seen Biggles at the same time. His voice broke off abruptly. And thus, for a long second, the scene remained, immobile, frozen, as it were, like a screen play suddenly arrested. Then, as if wondering at the sudden cessation of sound, the bowed heads were raised. The agents looked at their chief. They saw his fixed expression and noted the direction of his stare. With one accord they turned.

Biggles' gun slid into his hand and came up like the head of a striking cobra. 'Don't move, anybody,' he snapped. He would have avoided bloodshed had it been possible.

It was not. Perhaps the agents did not understand. Be that as it may, the words broke the spell. The order was ignored. Movement returned, and it returned with a rush. With a unanimous gasp of alarm, and a crashing of overturning chairs, the agents sprang to their feet in panic. In doing this they came between Biggles and Larapindi, who was not slow to seize the opportunity this human cover provided. He sprang to the wall, and on the instant the room was plunged into darkness.

Three streams of orange sparks leapt across the room. They started at the muzzle of Biggles' gun and ended at the spot where he had last seen Larapindi. Loud cries of fear accompanied the reports. There were answering shots from different points of the room, to be followed instantly by the thump of falling bodies. A little light entered through the open door from the hall, but it was not sufficient to enable Biggles to see clearly what was happening, except that all was in confusion. Men were staggering about, colliding with each other and falling over the chairs. It was a situation for which he was not prepared, and one that seemed to defy immediate remedy. He had no desire to perpetrate a massacre. Realising that he could serve no useful purpose by remaining inside the room, and that there was a chance of his being knocked down in the mêlée, he backed into the hall. It seemed to be the wisest course, particularly as he had only to keep the door covered from the outside to prevent anyone from escaping. On the spur of the moment he assumed this; and it was no doubt a natural assumption; but in the event it turned out to be another mistake. He took up a position in the lighted hall on one side of the door, few paces from it, and shouted at Ginger to take up a similar position on the other side.

'Plug anybody who tries to get away,' he ordered grimly.

'What a mess,' muttered Ginger in a disgusted voice, as he obeyed. He side-stepped briskly as a little brown man darted out, blazing wildly with a small automatic.

Biggles fired and the man went down. 'I'm afraid we've started something,' he said, with a worried frown, as from somewhere in the lower regions there came a crashing and banging, with a few sporadic shots.

'That must be our crowd breaking in—they've heard the rumpus,' opined Ginger. 'Why not lock the door, and keep Larapindi and the rest inside until the police come to collect them?' he suggested, indicating the room, from which now came an excited muttering.

'That's an idea,' agreed Biggles. He went to the door, and having taken the key from the far side, slammed it. He turned the key.

While this brief operation was in progress other things were happening. Algy put his head round the laboratory door and demanded to be told what was going on. Biggles gave him a brief idea of what had happened, and ordered him to remain where he was. Voices were shouting somewhere below. Feet thumped on stairs.

'Bigglesworth! Where are you?' called one voice.

'That sounds like Raymond,' said Ginger. 'What's he doing here?'

'He must have followed us—like an old hound that won't be left out of the hunt,' answered Biggles, smiling. 'Perhaps it's as well. I'll hand this mess over to him.'

Tug, gun in hand, appeared at the head of the stairs. There was blood on his face and on the front of his tunic. 'Have you got 'em?' he asked excitedly.

'Not exactly,' replied Biggles. 'What have you been up to?'

'I met a bloke on the stairs,' explained Tug. 'He tried to stop me coming up. We had a row about it and he got the worst of it.'

Air Commodore Raymond, panting heavily, was the next to arrive. 'What on earth are you doing here?' he demanded.

'I might ask you that,' returned Biggles curtly. 'I told you to keep out of it, so that—'

'I know. So that if things went wrong you could shoulder the blame. I'm not having that. I brought you out, so if anyone is going to get a rap it will be me.'

'It may come to that,' declared Biggles. 'Larapindi is a big bug in this part of the world, and he may be

179

able to pull enough strings to cause serious trouble in India. But we can talk about that later. Larapindi is the boss of the local spy ring — I've got all the evidence I need to prove that. He's in that room with some of his gang.'

'Then let's have him out,' said the Air Commodore bluntly.

'Okay,' agreed Biggles. 'But someone's liable to get hurt. I wanted to avoid that. I'm by no means sure of the nationality of some of these fellows, and we don't want to have a political issue made out of it. Still . . .' He went to open the door, turned the key, and pushing the door open, stepped inside. 'Come out of that,' he ordered. 'The place is surrounded. You can't get away.'

There was a brief pause. Then, one by one, four men came out.

'These men may be dressed like Hindus, but if they aren't Japs I'll eat my buttons,' swore the Air Commodore.

'Where are the rest?' said Biggles. The beam of his torch cut a wedge into the darkness of the room. He ran in and switched on the light. Three men were lying on the floor. Larapindi was not among them. Biggles' eyes flashed round the room. There was only one possible hiding-place — a large safe that stood open. He went to it and looked inside, but the man he sought was not there.

'He's got away,' he rasped. 'There must be a secret way out of this room — probably a lift. It's no use looking for it now.' He turned to the Air Commodore. 'I'll leave you to take care of things here, sir. Algy's in the next room with some things you ought to see. Tug, you stay here with Ginger and give the Air Commodore a hand to clean up the mess. He'll need some help.'

Biggles made for the stairs.

Chapter 17
The End of the Trail

Biggles went down the stairs three at a time, not a little annoyed at the turn the affair had taken—annoyed with himself, that is, for not having taken more direct action in the room upstairs. He should, he thought, have foreseen the possibility of the move Larapindi had made; for should the chief enemy agent escape, the coup he had planned would have to be accounted a failure. There was a chance that Larapindi might still be somewhere in the building, and if that were so, by posting the rest of the squadron to cover the exits, his escape might be frustrated.

He nearly fell over a body that lay at the foot of the second-floor staircase—presumably the man Tug had shot on his way up. Biggles turned his torch on him, and caught his breath sharply when it revealed a Japanese Air Force tunic. It was not until later, though, that he grasped the full significance of this. At the moment he was simply astonished that an enemy airman should wear uniform in such a place and at such a time. Without giving the matter serious thought, it flashed into his mind that the Japanese might possibly be one of those who had baled out in the combat, and had made his way under cover of dark to the warehouse, knowing that Larapindi would provide him with a hiding-place. The man still clutched in his hand a Japanese general service pattern revolver.

Biggles ran on down to the main hall. The first thing he saw was a man in native dress—the hall porter, he thought—lying on his back on the floor. A knife lay beside him. Taffy Hughes, as pale as death, sat in a chair, one foot in a pool of blood, with Johnny Crisp, on his knees, twisting a tourniquet round his leg.

'What's happened here?' asked Biggles sharply.

Johnny answered: 'Taffy and I bust the door in when the shooting started. Taffy was first. This guy—' Johnny indicated the man on the floor '—stuck a knife in him.'

'Look after him,' ordered Biggles. 'Have you seen a man go out through this door?'

'No one has gone out this way,' replied Johnny.

'Where are the others?'

'Outside, I suppose. Only Tug followed us in, and he went on up the stairs.'

Biggles went out into the street. The lorry was there, with Ferocity, alone, in charge.

'Have you seen a man come out of the building?' asked Biggles tersely.

'Not a soul,' returned Ferocity.

'Where's Bertie and Tex?'

'They went down the side street to grab Larapindi's car.'

'Okay. Stand by,' commanded Biggles. 'Taffy's been knifed, but Johnny is with him. If it turns out that Taffy is badly hurt you'll have to run him to the hospital. If not, wait for the others.'

Biggles ran on down the side street. Larapindi's car was still there. Tex, gun in hand, was standing beside it. The native driver cowered against the wall with his hands up.

'Have you seen anybody come out, Tex?' asked Biggles.

'Sure,' answered Tex. 'A little feller in European clothes shot out of the side door. When we shouted to him to stop he had a crack at us and then bolted towards the river. Bertie went after him.'

Biggles raced on down the street. It ended abruptly at the river, but to the right there was a long wharf, flanking the rear of the warehouse. 'Bertie! Where are you?' he shouted.

The answer was two pistol shots in quick succession. The reports came from the far end of the wharf, which was occupied by cranes, conveyors, trollies and similar dock equipment. Biggles ran towards the sound. More shots guided him as he ran. Then came another sound, one that spurred him to a sprint. It was the throbbing hum of a powerful motor-boat. He came upon Bertie taking long distance shots at a long low craft that was tearing the surface off the water as it headed up-stream.

'The blighter's got away,' muttered Bertie. 'Sorry, old boy.'

'Was he a little fellow in European clothes, wearing spectacles?'

'Yes. I lost sight of him in all this clutter. Next thing I saw was the boat.'

'Are there any more boats?' asked Biggles.

'I haven't seen any. I shouldn't think there are two like that.' Bertie pointed to the fast disappearing speed-boat. 'Let's follow in the car,' he suggested. 'The blighter's got to come ashore somewhere sooner or later,'

Biggles clicked his fingers. 'My gosh!' he muttered, aghast. 'I've just remembered something. I'll bet I know where he's making for. He's got an aircraft up the river. He's going to pull out.' Biggles went on quickly. 'We've still a chance. Bertie, go into the main hall and call Dum Dum on the 'phone; tell them to bring a Spit out and have it started up. I shall be there in five minutes.'

Without waiting to see if Bertie followed Biggles

raced back to Larapindi's car. 'Look out! I want this car,' he told Tex in a brittle voice. 'Take your prisoner inside and hand him over to Johnny. Tell Johnny to call an ambulance from the airfield to pick up Taffy. Then join Ferocity in the lorry and try to overtake a motor-boat that's heading up-stream. Larapindi's in it. He's got a hangar somewhere up the river, with a machine in it. Try to stop him from getting away. If the hangar is this side of the river you may have a chance.'

Biggles was moving as he spoke, and by the time he had finished he was in the driving-seat. The car shot forward, and in another minute was racing along the road to Dum Dum.

In the short drive that followed Biggles took risks which in the ordinary way he would have considered unjustifiable. The driver of a belated bullock cart, which he missed by inches in avoiding a careless pedestrian, would doubtless have agreed with him. But everything depended on speed. He reached the airfield without mishap, and after skidding to a standstill at the main gate to announce his identity, went straight on across the landing-field to where a Spitfire was standing, its engine idling.

'Is she all right, flight-sergeant?' he shouted to the N.C.O. in charge, as he jumped out.

'Okay, sir,' was the answer.

Biggles climbed into the cockpit. An instant later the engine roared and the Spitfire moved forward. In five seconds it was in the air, swinging round in a wide turn towards Calcutta. The river came into view. Biggles eased the control column forward. On reaching the river he turned steeply, and roared up-stream with the floor of his fuselage not more than fifty feet above the water. He noted several cars outside the warehouse

184

as he flashed past. Ahead, all he could see was that the placid surface of the river had been disturbed. There was no sign of the motor-boat. He tore on for three or four minutes, annihilating distance. Before him the moon gleamed on the broad surface of the water. He had always realised the futility of trying to make any sort of search in the dock area, which stretches for miles, but he hoped that somewhere above it, where there was less congestion of vessels, he would see either the motor-boat, or the aircraft. He saw neither. Doubts assailed him. It was only assumption that Larapindi would try to effect his escape by air. The enemy agent had asserted that the Gull was grounded for the duration; and so, undoubtedly, it had been—officially, Biggles reflected. But that would not prevent Larapindi from keeping it in an airworthy condition if he thought there was a chance that he might need it.

Biggles zoomed. Banking gently, his eyes probed the deep blue void through which he moved. He began to circle, extending his range with each turn. There was no sign of the aircraft he sought. Moodily he began to wonder if he had been wise in rushing into the air; and he was still wondering, torn by indecision, when during a turn he saw two bright sparks of light on the ground, winking at him. He took the lights to be the headlamps of a car, on the far bank of the river. With quickening interest he realised that this might be a signal to him, bearing in mind that the lorry would be able to judge his position by the sound of his motor.

Making for the lights he nearly collided with the Gull, and thereby had what must have been one of the narrowest escapes of his career. He did not know it was the Gull. He barely saw it. He was concentrating his attention on the winking headlights, trying to make out if the flashes formed a signal in Morse, when the thing happened. To say that a shadow appeared in the darkness would convey only a poor impression of the actual event. When two high-performance aircraft are approaching each other head-on, even in broad daylight, from the moment they become visible to each other, to the moment of contact, is a very short time indeed. At night the time factor is lessened, in ratio with reduced visibility. The black shape of the Gull did undoubtedly approach, but from the time it came into sight, to the moment of passing, was a split second. Biggles hardly saw it. Rather did he become aware of it. He acted without conscious thought. It was one of those occasions, and there are many in every pilot's career, when there is literally no time for thought. Life depends on perfect co-ordination of brain and limb. The two things, actuated by an impulse which is akin to instinct, must operate simultaneously, or all is lost. Biggles' right hand and foot jerked. The Spitfire reacted convulsively, like a horse startled from sleep. The two shadows seemed to merge. Then they flashed past each other. The danger was averted. Again Biggles moved. His nerves were rigid from shock, the sensation as when we say our heart stands still; but he moved. The control column was back in his thigh, and the Spitfire had whirled round almost in its own length. Then for the first time he really saw the Gull, and recognised it.

The rest was comparatively easy. Glancing down to see where he was he observed that by an ironic twist of fate the Gull was just passing over the eastern boundary of the airfield, from which the enemy agents had sent so many British pilots to their deaths. He waited for a moment and then fired a short burst past the Gull's cabin. He assumed that the civil machine would be unarmed, and he resolved to give the pilot a chance to land should he prefer surrender to death, although it would probably come to the same thing in the end. He did not think his enemy would accept the invitation. And he was right. The Gull jinked, and then, to Biggles' surprise, someone in the cabin opened fire on him with a machine-gun, presumably a mobile weapon. He hesitated no longer. Swinging round to the off-side quarter of the fugitive he closed in, took careful aim, and fired. Tracer flashed across the intervening distance. The apex of the cone of fire struck the Gull amidships; the machine appeared first to crumple, and then break across the cabin. Pieces broke off and whirled away astern. The nose of the stricken machine dropped. It dived. The motor was cut, but still it dived, in an ever-steepening swoop earthward. With expressionless face Biggles watched it strike the edge of a paddy-field. He circled twice and then turned away, not feeling inclined to risk a night landing near the wreck, although the country was open. In any case, he knew that there was nothing he could do for whoever might be in the machine. So he cruised back to the airfield and landed, taxi-ing on to the ambulance station.

'I've just shot an enemy machine down, not far from the road, about two miles east of the airfield,' he announced. 'I fancy there are casualties. I'll come with you.'

'I thought I heard shooting, sir,' answered the driver, as Biggles got in beside him.

There were two bodies in the wreck. One was Larapindi. The other, obviously the pilot, was unknown to him. The ambulance returned to the airfield and the bodies were taken to the mortuary. Biggles went back to Larapindi's car, which still stood where he had abandoned it, and drove quietly back to the warehouse.

Things were different from when he had left. A line of police cars occupied the kerb outside the main entrance, from which he gathered that the Air Commodore had considered it advisable to call for assistance. He found a little crowd in the hall; it included most of the members of the squadron, and the Air Commodore. His arrival caused a stir.

'What about Larapindi?' asked the Air Commodore urgently, anxiously.

'He won't give any more trouble,' answered Biggles.

'Where is he?'

Biggles took out his cigarette case. 'What's left of him is in the station mortuary,' he replied.

'How did that happen?'

'He'd got an aircraft parked up the river, apparently with a tame pilot standing by. He must have kept the machine there for just such an emergency.'

'We've found five Japanese airmen here so far, hiding in different parts of the building,' put in the Air Commodore. 'This must have been a rendezvous for enemy pilots who were forced down on our side of the lines. It seems that that was another of Larapindi's activities. The search is still going on. I take it you shot him down?'

'I had to, or he'd have got away. He was heading east. That's all there was to it. What's happened here?'

'Nothing very exciting, since you left. We're still cleaning up. We've taken everybody into custody. That stuff in the laboratory was interesting, but not so interesting as the contents of Larapindi's safe. You caught him on one foot, so to speak; otherwise, if he had had time, no doubt he would have destroyed everything. As it is, we've got particulars of the dope operatives on the other stations, to say nothing of other agents, and where they are working. They are being rounded up. By dawn the whole organization should be wiped out.'

'Was Larapindi a Jap,' asked Biggles.

'I haven't been able to get to the bottom of that yet,' answered the Air Commodore. 'He was a Fascist, anyway. He was a wealthy man, but that wasn't enough. He wanted power, which is an obsession with a certain type. I found a document in the safe, a sort of agreement, promising him a high political position in India should the country be taken by Japan. He played for a big stake, and lost.'

Biggles nodded. 'Have you found any indication as to whether this dope business was his own idea, or whether he was put up to it by Japan?'

'We don't know yet. We may never know—not that it's important.'

'What's the position of the firm?' queried Biggles.

'Oh, it was genuine enough, originally, there's no doubt of that,' asserted the Air Commodore. 'Larapindi was the crook. With Tahil out of the way it provided a wonderful background for espionage. The firm has agents and branches everywhere, and the top floor of this warehouse must have been an ideal meeting-place for enemy agents. Tahil died from snake-bite, you know.'

'So Laripindi told me. I should say Larapindi was the snake that bit him.'

'Old Tahil was a good fellow. It must have suited Larapindi to have him out of the way. Young Tahil, the old man's son, is at Oxford. I imagine he'll come back and take over the firm. Well, you've done a good job, Bigglesworth. I'll see you get credit for it.'

'You mean, you'll see that the squadron gets credit for it,' corrected Biggles.

The Air Commodore smiled. 'Of course—that's what I meant. I suppose you'd like to get back to England now? If you go right away I'm afraid you'll leave

Mackail and Harcourt here.'

'How are they? Have you heard lately?'

'Yes, I rang up the hospital this evening. Harcourt is doing fine—he wasn't seriously hurt. Mackail has come round, and the M.O. says he'll recover, but it will be some time before he flies again.'

'Good. What about Taffy? The last I saw of him he was sitting here bleeding like a pig. One of Larapindi's men had knifed him.'

'It's nothing serious,' stated the Air Commodore. 'In fact, Crisp, who went back with him in the ambulance, tells me that the M.O., after putting a stitch or two in him, has let him go to his quarters.'

'Bertie and Tex saw Larapindi take off,' put in Ginger, who was one of those standing by, listening to the conversation. 'They went with Ferocity in the lorry. they couldn't do anything to stop him because they were on the wrong side of the river.'

'Absolutely,' declared Bertie. 'All I could do was wink my jolly old headlights at you, to show you where we were.'

Biggles smiled. 'I saw them; and I was so interested in them that I nearly flew into Larapindi. If he was more scared than I was he must have died from shock. I shall have a nightmare to-night—the thought of collision always did give me the jitters.' He yawned. 'Which reminds me, a spot of sleep wouldn't do us any harm. Let's get back. I want to have a little wager with Taffy.'

'What is it?' asked Algy.

Biggles laughed. 'I'm going to bet him that the hole in my arm is deeper than the one in his leg. Come on. Let's go, before the Air Commodore thinks of another tangle for us to straighten out.'